- - - - -

By shedding a light on the difficult topics depicted in the following stories, my hope is that this book can help readers start a conversation about their struggles with mental health issues. I also hope to help others realize the struggle those with mental health issues go through and allow them to better help those in their life who may struggle.

If you are struggling with these issues yourself, this book may include triggering events and moments. You may want to consider reading it with your safe person.

I encourage struggling readers to reach out to a parent, friend, school counselor, an adult they trust, your safe person.

PART 0:
HENRY HOVISHKY
PRESENT DAY

- - - - -

As he took his last draw off an already burnt out cigarette and sipped the last bit of vodka and cranberry off the ice in his glass, Henry Hovishky got up to go inside for the night. He felt the cool breeze of the night flow across his face. His high and tight haircut and short and tapered beard held no protection from the cold. He felt a chill run down his short and stocky body. He shivered and blew into his hands to warm himself, but to no avail. Henry had been outside on the porch for the better part of two hours, reflecting on his life up to this point.

He had graduated from college only three years ago, yet he had already made waves in the community. He started off as a part-time financial planner and quickly moved up into a full-time job as the chief financial officer for a nationwide pharmaceutical development company. Recently, he had been named Young Professional of the Year by three different organizations around his community. He served on nonprofit boards and was well respected by nearly everyone in the community. His life had, seemingly, been a success.

He was successful now- building a house for his fiancé and himself and working his dream job. He had two of the best friends anyone could ask for and had a loving and supportive family. But it hadn't been an easy journey. He had fought many mental health issues for going on seventeen years now, undiagnosed until five years ago. He always knew he was different as a kid, but never knew how. His constant feelings of sadness, his constant moments of pain, his desire-turned-obsession to have everything JUST right, his angry outbursts all made sense when he was diagnosed.

He suffered from several mental health issues, including severe anxiety, bipolar disorder, and depression. It was a lot for one person to deal with, and he had fought through it with pills and alcohol to numb the pain and ease the worry. He fought through it without anyone and with no one understanding what was going on. He fought through it with thoughts of suicide to stop hurting. Through all the fighting, he came out alive with only a few battle scars.

As he opened the door to go inside, he heard the pitter-patter of his dog Dutch coming around the corner. Dutch was a beautiful mix with the muscular body, cedarwood coloring, and curled tail of a German Shepard. He had the best innocent puppy dog eyes and held the set of strong legs reminiscent of a lab. Dutch looked up at him, his tail wagging, his spotted tongue stuck out, and a dog's version of a smile creeping around his mouth. Dutch ran out the door, past Henry, and took a long stretch, shaping his body like a crescent moon.

The night sky looked like Las Vegas at Midnight- dark, but full of life. The sky was a pitch black, but the stars twinkled like lightning bugs flying through the sky. It was a perfect night and he had taken the next day off work. Henry closed the door, turned around, and sat back down in his chair.

He grabbed the bottle of vodka and cranberry juice he kept in the freezer outside and refilled his glass to the brim. He lit another cigarette out of his lonesome pack, the embers shining among the stars. He heard Dutch coming back on the porch and he curled up at Henry's feet. Again, he reflected on his life and his journey. The journey of his battles, his bouts, and the life he lived.

PART 1:
MICHELLE & JOE WEST
FIVE YEARS AGO

- - - - -

Henry walked out the glass door of his doctor's office, the sun blinding him as he stepped onto the concrete. He hated going to the doctor's office, it was dark and smelled of sickness. The somber mood that always seemed to lurk in the waiting room made Henry's anxiety soar.

He stood there for a minute with his hand shielding his eyes, waiting for them to adjust to the bright, beautiful day from the dim and poorly lit doctor's office. He walked to a candy red Ford Mustang, opened the door, and slowly fell into the driver's seat. He rested his head against the steering wheel, breathing in deep gulps of air. His mind was racing with a thousand different thoughts, as he tried to find the words to describe how he felt.

"I can't believe it," Henry thought to himself, grabbing his right shoulder. *"I just can't believe it."*

He picked up his phone and looked down at the picture of his favorite athlete, David Ortiz, staring back at him. "I bet you didn't have to deal with this kind of shit," he said aloud as he went to his recent calls. He found the contact he was looking for- a contact whose number he should know by heart.

"Hello?" a beautiful, soothing woman's voice sang through the other end of the phone.

"Mom, its Henry." Michelle West was a beautiful woman with long dark hair in her late thirties. She had been the lighthouse through his stormy life, guiding him through the rough sea to try and bring him to shore. "I'm leaving the doctor's office," he finished.

"Well, sweetie, what did they say?"

"I don't understand," he quietly said into the phone.

Michelle recognized his tone of despair and responded, "Henry, what's wrong? What did they say?"

"Mom, I just don't get it. It's not fair. It's not fair!" he exclaimed.

"You have to talk to me, tell me what's going on."

Henry took in a deep breath. He was trying to find words again, not knowing what to say. He had this problem for nearly his entire life, when push came to shove, he struggled to find the words he needed to say. People often thought he was cold or emotionless because of his loss of words when his emotions hit him like a snow flurry.

"They told me I have a whole lot of issues. Issues that people shouldn't have to deal with. Things that just make me feel… awful," Henry finally managed to say.

"What kind of issues?"

"Anxiety, bipolar, depression. I'm not normal, Mom. I'm not a normal person. I'm a freak. I'm going to have to be on medicine for the rest of my life to try and be normal!"

"Henry, you are NOT a freak. Nobody is normal in this world. Nobody is perfect. There is no such thing as 'normal'."

"Maybe, but I'm full of problems and issues, they could put me on the cover of Time magazine with all of my issues! It explains why I am the way I am, why I have always been sad and angry and just plain crazy."

"You aren't crazy, honey. You're unique, you were built by God to be a warrior. He wanted you to be able to fight these battles and rise up on the other side to show the world your strength. You know I love you and I always will."

Henry's mom always knew what to say. Somehow, someway, she could ease the pain and lift the burden that would settle on his shoulders. He reached to his right shoulder and put his hand on the tattoo he got for his mom, a lighthouse with waves crashing around it to form a heart. Sometimes, to calm himself down, he would close his eyes, grab that shoulder, and remember her and all that she had done to help him get where he was.

"Thank you, Mom. I love you," Henry whispered.

"I love you Henry. What did the doctor say about medications?" Michelle asked.

"She said it's going to be a process. Everyone reacts differently to different medications. She's going to start me off on one type, and I'll follow up in a month and we'll go from there."

"Just remember sweetie, if any of the medicines make you feel worse you need to try and get in sooner." Michelle said, her mind focused on her son. "We'll be here for you to help you along the way."

"I know, I know. I'll talk to you later Mom," Henry said as he reluctantly hung up the phone. He didn't want to hang up, but his emotions were welling up and he didn't want his mom to have to hear this.

Henry put his head back against the steering wheel of his car and slowly put the key in the ignition. The quiet ding of the car coming to life filled the hallows of the silent car, ringing in Henry's ears like a siren at sea. He couldn't focus with the noise racking around in his skull. He felt a faint throbbing beginning in his temples, working its way around his head. Grabbing the sides of his head with his index fingers, Henry slowly began rubbing his temples to ease the pain of the oncoming migraine.

- - - - -

While Michelle sat at her work desk the next day, her mind began to swirl and wander back to her son. He hadn't come by the night before, which wasn't unusual, but it still made her heart hurt. Michelle couldn't help but to feel partially at fault for what was going on with her son. Of course, she knew there was nothing she actually did that caused him to feel the ways he does, but her maternal instinct made her care and worry more and more.

There was a rapid knock at Michelle's office door. "Come in," Michelle answered to the knock. The door slowly opened to reveal her husband, Joe, with a bouquet of flowers and a grin on his face.

"Happy anniversary," Joe smiled at her. Joe was a taller man, with an average build. He had dirty blonde hair, and scraggly facial hair rounding out his chin. Joe came into Michelle's life when Henry was just seven years old but had treated him and his brother Leonard like they were his own.

Michelle had gotten lucky with this man, after the disaster that was her first husband.

"You're so sweet. Thank you, Joe.," Michelle gave a halfhearted smile towards Joe, not meaning to take her frustrations out on him.

Joe, instantly noticing her gloomy look responded "What's wrong? What's bothering you?"

"No, I'm fine. What did you have planned? You didn't come all the way out here just to bring me flowers," she said jokingly with a loving smile afterwards.

"Get up," Joe said, grabbing his wife's coat off the coat rack by the door. "We're going to Driftwood Café." Michelle got up and walked towards the door, as Joe helped her with her jacket.

As Michelle rode shotgun in Joe's truck, she found herself staring out the window. She couldn't help but to think about her oldest son and the way he must be feeling after he received, what he believed to be, a life-changing diagnosis. Michelle understood that the diagnosis *could* be life changing, and it probably would be for Henry. She had been diagnosed with severe anxiety years ago, remembering how she felt after her doctor had told her that. *"Henry must feel so defeated right now,"* Michelle thought to herself.

As the clouds rolled by in the sky, the sun beaming down trying to illuminate Michelle's gloomy face, she began to think back on Henry's childhood. He had been a quiet child. He had a few friends in those years, but always seemed to keep to himself. He constantly compared himself to other kids, his brother, or his cousins and would say things like *"I'll never be as good as them,"* or *"I'm sorry I can't do things like them,"* and every time he said that it would break her heart. One of the things Michelle remembered the most, however, was his obsession with death. It was hard for her to remember these things, but after talking to Henry it was overtaking her mind.

Henry never talked about wanting to die, but he was obsessed with the concept of death. He constantly asked questions about dying and would have thoughts about what death was and why it happened. Often, he would wake up in the middle of the night and go into Michelle and Joe's room in tears, asking them *"What happens when you die? What happens to the people in your life after you die?"* However, one of the concepts he obsessed over the most was *"Why do we work our whole lives, only to die and lose it all?"*

The signs had been there throughout his childhood, but Michelle had missed them. Had she missed them, or had she subconsciously ignored them? She didn't want her son to suffer from depression. Had she thought if she ignored them, they would go away, and he wouldn't suffer anymore?

As the thoughts flew around in Michelle's head, she felt the truck come to a stop. "You ready?" Joe asked, looking over at Michelle as she gazed out of the window. Without saying anything, Michelle slowly opened the door and got out of the truck. Joe, confused, followed her lead as they went into the café.

Joe and Michelle sat down at a table situated in the furthest corner of the café, away from the rest of the customers. A young waitress brought them a set of menus and two waters to get them started. While Joe looked down at his menu, he noticed Michelle hadn't moved a muscle since sitting down. She sat still and quiet, with her head resting in her hands, the same distant gaze she had in the truck beaming from her eyes. "Michelle, please tell me what's wrong," Joe pleaded.

"It's Henry," Michelle whispered in a hushed tone.

"What's wrong with him?" Joe asked, panicked. He hadn't seen Michelle like this since Henry had moved out of their house last year. He loved Henry and missed him too, but Joe had a different way of expressing it than Michelle.

"He went to the doctor yesterday, I guess he finally decided he needed to see someone about his mood swings," Michelle began. "He told me they diagnosed him with more than just depression. They told him he had anxiety and bipolar disorder on top of depression. I'm just worried about him Joe, he's my baby boy and he was so upset on the phone yesterday."

"Are they sure? I mean, don't you think he should go get a second opinion before getting on all of those medications? I can *maybe* see the depression, but the rest I just don't know."

"No, Joe, I think it's all very likely. He's shown signs for it all his life, I just didn't WANT to see them. I feel like I let him down, and..."

"Michelle," Joe interjected. "You have not let him down. He knows that. The boy loves you and looks up to you. You've been such a great mom, and everybody sees that." Joe reached across the table and gently took Michelle's hands in his. "We will help Henry through this. That's our boy, and we won't let him down."

"His depression… I can tell it's getting worse. And the way he sounded yesterday. This news. It was eating away at him. I'm worried about him."

Joe slowly got up, letting Michelle's hands drift down to the table. He went and sat in the seat next to her, putting his arm around her shoulder and pulled her close. "Henry's a fighter. He will fight through this. WE will all fight through this, together."

Michelle smiled as she nuzzled her nose in between Joe's chest and forearm. She took a deep breath, breathing in the smell of his woody cologne- a scent mixed with a hint of vanilla and sandalwood. Joe's smell had a way of calming Michelle down when she was upset, and it was just one of the many reasons she loved him.

- - - - -

As Joe pulled away from his wife's office, he looked in his rearview mirror to see her waving bye to him. His wife was beautiful, sweet, caring, and most importantly, a great mother. He knew it hurt to know her son was in pain, and it hurt him to know it too. Henry had always been a great kid. Smart. The kind to give 110% towards anything he wanted.

Joe wasn't sure what he was getting into, dating a girl with kids. He was a country boy from the next county over when he had met Michelle. She was a young, single mother, who loved her kids more than life itself. However, it turned out to be one of the best decisions of his life, learning to love and be a father to her two kids. He never viewed himself as a father until those kids came into his life, but he wouldn't have it any other way now.

It was hard at first for him to connect with Henry. Henry wasn't really into sports like Joe was, and Joe didn't enjoy learning like Henry did. However, the two were able to bond over a shared love: Hunting. He remembered the feeling of seeing Henry tag his first deer, and a smile crept across his own face. It was Joe's first real 'proud dad' moment.

Joe's mind shifted back to what Michelle had told him about Henry. He couldn't stop thinking about him and how he must be feeling. It was hard for him to wrap his head around the concept of depression and being on medicine for something like that. Growing up, Joe was taught that a man should just power through his problems. He knew that wasn't Henry's upbringing, though. He wanted to reach out and help him but just didn't know how.

Joe picked up his phone and dialed his wife's number. "Hello?" her voice rang from the other end of the line.

"Michelle, I've been thinking about Henry ever since we talked," Joe began. "How can we help him? What do we need to do to help him? I don't want him to feel like he's alone. I want him to know that we will always be on his side, fighting through this with him."

"I don't know Joe, I really don't. I want to reach out to him, but I don't want him to feel like we're treating him differently now."

Joe knew his wife was right. Henry would feel like he was being treated differently if they just continually reached out to him without reason. How could they reach out to him without making him feel different? How could they make him know that he isn't alone in this journey? What could they do?

"Joe?" His wife questioned. He had been silent for longer than he noticed.

"Sorry Michelle. I'm just thinking. Trying to figure out how we can help him without adding to the problem. It isn't easy."

"I know it isn't. That's what worries me. If we come off as overbearing and he feels like we are treating him differently, then he feels like he is a burden to us and gets upset. We wait for him to reach out to us and don't make an effort, he feels like he's alone and nobody cares. It's a catch twenty-two. He's my son, If I could take the pain and hurt from him and give it to me, I would."

"He's OUR son Michelle, and I want to take it away from him too. We're going to figure this out. We're going to help Henry, and be there for him," Joe said, confidently.

"Thank you, Joe, for loving Henry and Leonard like you do. I couldn't ask for a better dad for the kids. They love you so much, and I love you."

"I love them with my life, and I love you. I'll see you tonight," Joe said as he hung up the phone.

Joe pulled onto the long dirt road that led to his home. As he drove down the road, with the dust coming from his tires filling the air like a cloud behind him, a deer ran out in front of Joe causing him to slam on the brakes.

The truck slid from side to side as Joe tried to come to a stop on the dry, dirt road.

When the truck finally came to a full stop, Joe looked up to see the deer standing nearly a foot from his truck. The deer and Joe locked eyes as Joe tried to catch his breath. Joe couldn't help but to examine the deer: a majestic twelve-point buck; the cleanest white antlers he'd ever seen on a deer; an almost flawless cedar wood colored coat; and bright, sky-blue eyes. There was something about the eyes on the deer that captivated Joe. He couldn't put his finger on what it was, he just couldn't turn away from the deer's gaze. It felt like they held a thousand secrets.

The bushes behind the deer began to rustle as two smaller fawn came out of the woods and began crossing the road. The elder deer didn't break his locked eyes from Joe until the two smaller completely crossed the road and disappeared back into the woods. *"Why did that deer just stand there and stare at me?"* Joe thought. Having been an avid hunter his whole life, he had never seen a deer stand its ground like that one had.

He picked up his phone and pulled up Henry's contact. *[Hey bud, you coming by tonight?]* he typed, looking up to see the back of the elder deer disappearing into the woods. Joe slowly lifted his foot off the brake and crept the truck back to his house. As he pulled into the driveway, he heard his phone ding.

Joe looked down at his phone to see a message from Henry reading *[Not sure. Lot of homework.]* That was Henry's typical excuse to not do something. He didn't doubt that Henry did have a lot of homework. Joe just knew his stepson all too well.

[Feel free to come by, mom's making meatloaf,] He sighed and opened the door of his truck, letting in a flood of sunlight. Joe put his hand over his eyes to shield them from the blinding sun as he walked to the door. He stopped as he got to the door and looked over into the woods to his left.

There was the same deer again, staring at him with those mysterious sky-blue eyes, with the two fawn standing behind him.

- - - - -

Henry laid his phone back on his night stand as he rolled over in bed to face the blank wall. Henry suspected his mom had already told Joe about what he found out yesterday, and he appreciated Joe reaching out. However, he felt like Joe was just trying to be nice. He didn't want to be a burden on his family, so he had decided that he should go over there as little as possible.

Henry thought about all the people in his life who had disappeared. He thought about his childhood friends that he no longer talked to and hadn't since they graduated high school. His mind drifted to the girl he dated in high school who had cheated on him multiple occasions. He remembered how his dad had abandoned him, mentally and physically, years ago. He couldn't help but to wonder if all those people had disappeared because of his issues. So many people had been there for him through moments of despair and anger, periods of solitude and sorrow, and every one of them were now gone. He couldn't blame them. People had their own problems to deal with and it wasn't fair to expect others to deal with his. He loved his mom and Joe, but he was afraid of driving them away with his presence and his constant sorrow.

His brightly lit room provided no distraction for Henry's sleepy eyes. As Henry dozed off into a deep sleep, his mind kept thinking about what he had found out. He tossed and turned in his bed, trying to shake the thoughts creeping into his mind. Through the rustling of his covers covering his head as he tossed and turned, Henry heard a slam come from outside his door. He leaped out of the bed, nearly tripping on his covers, and slowly opened his door-letting in a sudden darkness that surrounded him.

"How long was I asleep? It was daylight when I fell asleep," Henry thought to himself as he stepped out of his bedroom and looked around.

Then, the door slammed shut behind him. He turned to try and open his door, but the door knob was stuck and blazing hot. As he snatched his hand away from the door knob like a scorned dog, he turned back around and slowly realized he had no idea where he was. Darkness surrounded the space he had just walked into, his eyes slowly trying to adjust to the sudden blackness. Henry began to take baby steps through the darkness, feeling the walls for a light switch.

His eyes began to adjust to the darkness, but still all he could see were a few outlines of objects. Why was it so dark? Why did he not recognize his own apartment? What was going on?

Henry took a step forward, tripping on something in his way. His body collapsed to the floor, his face banging the cold ground beneath him. As he reached up to rub his nose, he felt a warm, sticky liquid all over his hands and face.

"Did I hit the ground so hard I'm bleeding?" Henry wondered as he rubbed his fingers together, trying to figure out what the liquid was.

Henry began to feel around for some kind of support to lift himself off the ground. He grabbed something behind him, something leaning against the wall. It was cold and leathery, and as Henry worked his hands up to the top of the mysterious object, his hands wrapped around a spherical object topping the support off, causing him to have a horrific realization. *"Oh shit, this is a body!"*

Henry stumbled to get up, clawing his way up the wall behind him and moving his own body away from the one next to him. He tried to scream out for help, but nothing came out., his mouth wouldn't open, and his vocal cords only made a muffled vibration. He tried to scream again. It was still useless. He felt like he had been overtaken by sleep paralysis, and he was awaiting the vision of an incubus to appear in front of his face.

As he got to his feet, he saw the outline of some type of figure slowly coming towards him. *"Is this what left the corpse?"* He wondered. *"What the fuck is going on."*

As the figure closed in on him, Henry tried to turn and run. He quickly realized, however, that his feet were stuck in a pool of the sticky liquid he had slipped in. The figure was within arm's reach of Henry now, and his fight or flight instincts kicked in. Henry attempted to swing at the figure, but his muscle locked in place and wouldn't move. *"Oh God. No."*

The figure was on top of Henry now, but he still couldn't make out who – or what – it was. It reached out with its hand and ran its fingernails down Henry's arms, causing blood to pour down his arms. The figure's cold breath beat down on Henry's face, causing a chill to rush through his body like an arctic blast. The closer it got, the harder it was for Henry to see anything around him. Henry closed his eyes, not knowing what to expect next.

"Henry," he heard a voice call.

Suddenly, the cold of its breath was gone, the pain of the scratching stopped, and Henry slowly opened his eyes. He was in his apartment again, slumped against the wall. He could see again; the darkness had disappeared from the space around Henry.

He looked over to his left, only to find the body still there that he had grabbed onto. The body, cold and lifeless, was slumped over. It was mangled, his arms spiraled. Henry reached over to lift the head of the lifeless body and see who it was.

As he saw who the body belonged to, he tried to scream again. He dropped the head of the body, its chin slamming back against its chest. He still couldn't yell out for help. *"How is this possible?"* Henry thought to himself, panicked. *"The body… it's me."* Henry felt like he was in a hall of mirrors. *"No. No. No! NO!"* Henry kept screaming in his head.

Henry's eyes shot open as he swatted the covers off his face and gasped for air. *"It was a dream,"* he thought to himself.

Henry took in deep breaths of the cold air sneaking in from his open window. He slid his legs off the bed, plopping them on the floor below. He lifted his weak body off the bed, still breathing in heavily, and walked into the kitchen.

"I need a drink," Henry said, opening a fifth of Wild Turkey Bourbon and pouring himself a glass. Henry believed that drinking was a 'cure-all' to his sadness and sorrow, drinking to numb the pain when it became too much. It was a habit he had picked up about a year ago, and even though he was only twenty now, he had so-called friends that had instilled this habit in him.

Henry sipped the bourbon off the ice and closed his eyes. He put his head back as he felt it burn as it flowed down his throat. The burn always seemed to burn away the pain, the sorrow, and the misery. In the darkness he saw the image of his mangled dead body. He saw the silhouette of the dark figure and felt the cold seeping into his pores. He heard the mysterious voice calling his name. His eyes shot open and he looked back down at his glass, now almost empty, and sat it on the counter. He reopened the bottle and took a straight shot. He made his way into the living room, where he plopped down on the couch and turned on the TV to the first show he found.

He tilted the bottle up to his lips, draining it between gulps of air. When the last drop was gone, and Henry's last breath encompassed the empty space where bourbon once sat, he slowly sat it down beside him realizing that he had just finished a fifth alone in less than an hour.

Henry, his vision now blurry and his coordination off, struggled to pull his phone out. His mind was craving affection now, craving sex. With a creepy smile making its way across his face, he sent the text every drunk person sends *[you up?]*

He sent the text to a girl named Jessica, who he had one-night stands with occasionally in the past. He and Jessica had hooked up after a long night of drinking a few months ago. Neither one of them wanted a relationship, but they both were obsessed with fucking. About once a week, one or the other would get drunk and text the other to come over.

Before he could even put his phone down, it dinged *[yea what's up?]*. Henry typed out a message asking her to come over and she responded with a simple *[ok.]*.

Half an hour later, Henry heard a knock at his door. He got up and stumbled to the door, after finishing the second fifth of whiskey he was finally feeling good. He opened the door and saw Jessica's round face, her brown hair sneaking down the left side, her grey eyes framed by a pair of glasses staring back at him.

"Come on in," Henry said with a drunken smile. Jessica walked through the door, it was a situation she was all too familiar with. There was something different about Henry this time, it was like someone else controlling him. She had never seen him this drunk before.

As Jessica and Henry made their way into his bedroom, Jessica noticed an empty fifth of bourbon sitting proudly on his counter. Ignoring this, she followed Henry into the room and then onto the bed. Henry, grabbing her hand, rolled on top of Jessica and began kissing her face. "Henry, stop," Jessica said.

Henry rolled back onto his side of the bed. He was frustrated, but even in his drunken stooper he knew no meant no. "What," he scowled.

"What's wrong with you? I've seen you drunk, but this is more than normal."

"Oh, sorry. Didn't know I called a therapist, thought I called a late-night booty call."

"Really Henry? We were friends before we ever started hooking up. I've seen you when you've been at your highest and at your lowest. I still care about you."

"No, you don't. You care about the one-night stands and that's it. Don't pretend you care," Henry lashed out.

"Henry! What is going on with you?"

"What's going on with me? I'm useless," Henry quietly whimpered. "I'm a piece of shit, who isn't going anywhere." Henry got out of the bed and walked to the wall, where he rested his head and slowly started pounding it against the wall.

"Henry, stop," Jessica whispered.

"NO!" He yelled back. "This whole life isn't worth living, everyone would be better off if I wasn't here! I make everyone around me miserable, and I'm sick of it!"

"Henry, please…."

Henry looked over to his whiteboard calendar where he kept his schedules and due dates. He felt his blood boiling as he looked at the dates scribbled in messy handwriting, the frustration of the work he had to do coming up, and the pure anger overcoming him. He ripped the calendar off the wall and slung it across the room, putting a hole in the wall. The plaster came crashing to the ground in several pieces.

"This is useless! I'm not going anywhere, I don't need this school shit. I'm not going anywhere anyways, I might as well drop out!" Henry yelled with anger-fueled tears falling down his cheeks. "I'm a nobody and that's all I'll ever be!"

"Henry, you're scaring me. Please, stop."

Henry looked over at Jessica, trembling with tears slowly welling up in her eyes. Henry put his back against the wall and gave up supporting his own weight. As his body made its way to the floor, his knees came to his chest and he wrapped his arms around his legs, burying his face in between his knees, and began to sob. He had made a fool of himself because he got drunk- or at least he told himself that was the reason. While he had said these things out of anger and in drunkenness, he surprised himself at how he truly meant every word that he had said.

Jessica got up from the bed and sat down beside Henry, put her arm around him, and rubbed his forearm. She didn't know what to do, she had never seen Henry like this. It had legitimately scared her, she wasn't sure what he was going to do next. "Henry, it's going to be okay. I don't know what's going on, but I'm here for you," she whispered to him as she put her head on his shoulder as he wept.

"You've got to go," Henry said in between deep breaths, attempting to calm himself down. "I don't know who I am anymore. You can't be here."

"Henry, I don't want to leave you here alone like this. Please, let me stay tonight," she pleaded.

"Why? Why would you want to be around someone like this? I'm a freak."

"Because I care," she said, pulling him closer.

"Leave." Henry said sternly. The late nights drinking, the meaningless sex they had with one another, the fact that they only talked when they wanted sex, it all reminded him of the bad decisions he continued to make for his selfish reason, and he wanted her to go. He also knew he couldn't keep putting her through this type of behavior.

"Henry, please…"

"Go."

- - - - -

Henry opened his eyes to the sun piercing through his curtains. His head was pounding and he felt sick to his stomach.

"I drank way too much last night," Henry thought to himself as he rolled over to check his phone. The simple light from his phone caused a pounding pain to circle through his head again.

One text message read, *[Henry, are you okay?]*. The message was from Jessica. Henry scrolled through the messages to see where he had invited her over last night. *"What the hell did I do?"*

Jessica had been his fling for the last few months, but it was a bad habit he was trying to break. They had been friends for years, but recently explored new territory with each other. They only talked when one or the other was drunk now. He felt bad that he had ruined such a good friendship with his need for companionship, but it was one of the things he had turned to fill the void.

He had a missed call and two texts from his mom. *[Missed u at dinner last night.]* and *[U ok? Tried calling.]* Henry felt bad for ignoring his mom and Joe, but knew it was what he had to do. He was tired of being a burden on those he loved, and he was tired of pushing them away because of it. This was his way of easing their pain.

Henry's phone began to ring, it was his mom again. He stared at the phone as his mom's name and picture appeared under 'incoming call'. He stared at the white letters against the black screen, conflicted on whether to answer the call or not. When the phone finally stopped ringing, Henry turned it off and buried his face in his pillow as he felt the tears building up from within.

- - - - -

Michelle looked at her phone as the robotic voice on the other side rattled off her son's phone number and finished by saying he wasn't available. She put her head down and sighed. She couldn't help but to worry. She felt her husband's warm touch on her back, as she lifted her head and laid it on his chest.

"Still haven't heard from Henry?" Joe asked, worriedly.

"No, he hasn't answered any of my calls or returned my texts over the last two weeks. Is he upset with me?" Michelle sighed.

"I highly doubt that, Michelle. He's probably sleeping still, you know that boy likes to sleep," Joe jokingly responded.

"You're probably right," Michelle said with a sigh. She couldn't help but to worry, it wasn't like Henry to not answer her calls for days in a row. She tried to focus on anything other than her worry, but she couldn't break that train of thought.

Michelle's own anxiety was getting the best of her. *"Is he mad at me? Is he okay? Does he know I love him? Is he hurting right now? He's hurting right now, I just know it. My poor baby, God why can't I take away his pain?"* She couldn't help but to wonder. Her mind was like a tornado taking all of her thoughts and spinning them around and around until they landed somewhere Michelle didn't want to be.

Her phone began to ring, and Michelle felt a bundle of hope jump into her chest. She swiftly reached down to grab her phone, but saw it was a number she didn't recognize. Once again, worry overcame her.

- - - - -

As Joe stood on his back porch, smoking a cigarette and playing a game on his phone, his mind wandered away from the present. Joe was worried about his wife and Henry. He knew they were both in pain. He wanted to help them, but he didn't know how and that's what frustrated him the most. He always liked to be the problem solver, the one in the family people could look to when they needed help.

He knew Henry was going through a rough time, and while he told Michelle he was probably still sleeping over the last week anytime she was worried about him not answering her calls, he was afraid he was being naïve. Henry did sleep in a lot, but for him to sleep until three in the afternoon and not return phone calls for days on end was unheard of. He looked down at his watch and saw the time was creeping on eight at night.

"Maybe I should try calling Henry." Joe thought to himself as he looked down at his phone, contemplating his next move.

All of a sudden, there was a rustle in the woods. Joe's head swiftly turned to look at the wood line. It was dark out that night, no stars and no moon shone in the night sky. He couldn't make anything out on the wood line. He ran inside and grabbed his flashlight, moving quickly to see what was in the woods. There had been a string of robberies throughout the neighborhood the last few weeks, and Joe was taking no chances.

As he ran back on the porch, he heard the rustle again. He flipped the switch of the light on and shined it on the wood line. Scanning the wood line like a prison guard, Joe couldn't find the cause of the noise.

He heard it again, this time closer to his home, and swung the light towards it. He caught the shine off an animal's eyes, staring at him. It looked like the same deer from earlier in the week, standing tall and proud with no fear of the man standing in front of it. The twelve tine on his head reflected the light from the moon as he appeared from the wood line like a spirit out the sky. The glowing eyes of the deer locked eyes with Joe, but there was something different about his eyes this time. They still held that

43

mysterious look to them, almost like they were trying to tell him something.

- - - - -

Henry was driving down a dark road, something he often did when his mind got the best of him. He would go to no destination in particular, he just drove the lonely road until he couldn't drive anymore. He couldn't stop thinking about the dream. He had it again. What could it have meant? Seeing himself, bloody and mangled, sent shivers down his spine. And that dark figure. Henry could still feel its cold breath on his face and its nails running down his arms.

Henry rubbed his arm, feeling a phantom pain. His mind kept racing, and he couldn't manage to get control of it. Everything was boiling over, and he just couldn't handle the pain anymore. His vision started to get blurry as his eyes began to tear up. He felt like his breath was escaping him and every time he tried to catch it, more got away from him.

44

The road began to curve sideways. As he drove, he felt like he was in a video game with the road swirling and collapsing around him. He was losing touch with reality, he almost didn't recognize where he was. His breaths were further and further apart. *"Just make it to Mom's, just make it to Mom's,"* he told himself over and over again.

- - - - -

Joe heard the roar of the Mustang echoing through the silence of the woods as Henry came down the dirt road. He looked over his shoulder to see headlights coming into the driveway. By the time he turned back around to see the deer, it had disappeared into the night as mysteriously as it had appeared.

Henry opened the door before he could even fully put it in park, stumbling out as his feet hit the ground. The car rocked back and forth. He felt like the air was being forced out of his lungs, a snake was crushing his chest, and his eyes were being plucked out of their sockets. He struggled to control his legs and make them move to get him inside the house.

Michelle heard the sound of Henry's Mustang pull into the driveway and the slam of his door as it closed behind him. *"Oh Henry, you came to see us!"* She thought joyfully, as she clapped her hands silently together. She half-walked and half-ran to the door to welcome Henry in, she hadn't talked to him in a days and missed him.

Joe saw Henry stumbling up the steps, like he was drunk. He knew Henry wouldn't drink and drive though, so what was wrong with him? "Henry, you okay?" Joe asked.

"He... Help. Mom. Can't... breathe," Henry gasped.

"Henry what's wrong," Joe said as he went to help him up the steps.

Henry couldn't talk anymore. He was afraid that his next breath would be his last. He just focused on moving his legs. The ground felt like it was slowly giving way beneath him. He knew he had to get inside where he could try to calm down.

Michelle saw her husband supporting her oldest son through the door, and her joy instantly turned to panic. "Joe, what's going on? What's wrong with Henry?" She frantically asked.

"I don't know Michelle, he pulled up and could barely get up the stairs. All he could say was help, asked for you, and said he couldn't breathe."

"Get him on the couch. We need to get him to calm down!"

As Joe laid Henry face up on the couch, he could hear the desperate gasps for air coming from his stepson's chest. He didn't know what to do, he put his hand over his mouth in an attempt to contain his fear. He had to walk back outside for a minute to catch his breath.

Michelle leaned over her son, her head on his chest, her hand holding onto his. She had never seen him have a panic attack, but she knew that had to be what it was. Her panic attacks had never been this bad, but the symptoms were similar. She put that out of her mind now as she kept her hands on her son and tried to stay calm

Henry couldn't see. He knew he must be at his mom's house, but he couldn't figure out exactly where he was in the house. He knew his eyes were open, feeling the burn of the dry air attacking his eyeballs, but everything was black. He was still gasping for air, he knew that for sure. His chest was slowly tightening its grip, causing an unbearable pain. His stomach was in a thousand knots as he struggled to breathe.

Joe walked back into the living room to see his wife leaning over Henry, her head on his chest, whispering "Just breathe, Henry. Just breathe." Joe walked over to the couch and got on his knees. He grabbed his wife's free hand and rubbed her back, and gently kissed her head.

Michelle felt her husband's warmth surround her and breathed in his scent. With the comfort of her husband surrounding her, she began to calm down. As she calmed down, she could feel Henry's chest palpitations begin to return to normal, and his gasps for air disappearing as his breathing returned to normal.

The light slowly started to come back into Henry's vision. He was beginning to find his breath again as his chest released the grip it held. His stomach slowly unwound. He saw the outline of his mother's head on his chest, and his stepdad comforting her. He made it. He made it home to his mom and Joe. Henry blinked a couple of times before speaking. "I'm sorry," Henry whimpered.

"Honey, please don't apologize," Michelle pleaded, with tears still sliding slowly down her blush face.

"I'm making y'all miserable. I'm adding stress to your lives. I'm sorry," Henry cried.

"Henry, stop. We love you son," Joe said calmly, all things considered.

"You can't love me, I'm unlovable," Henry felt the tears in his eyes welling up again. He hated feeling so useless.

"We love you, son," Michelle stammered, trying to hold her tears back.

"Henry, we want to help you. We want to be here for you," Joe said, still rubbing his wife's back and holding her hand.

"Why?" Henry managed to get out.

"You're our son," Michelle said looking over her shoulder at Joe. "We want you to know we are here for you, and we won't ever leave you. No matter how rough things are."

Henry managed to sit up, and buried his head in his mom's shoulder. Michelle wrapped her arms around her son, holding him tightly. Joe put his hands on his wife's shoulders and rested his face against the top of her head.

There they were, the three of them, encompassed in what they loved the most about each other.

Slowly, Henry started to understand that he would never drive Michelle and Joe away. Henry understood that they loved him because of his differences, not in spite of them.

PART 2:
WANDA & GEORGE HARE
FOUR YEARS AGO

- - - - -

Henry laid in the back of a cold ambulance, with a dim light beating on his face. His body was sore, his eyes filled with blood and sweat. A paramedic was standing over top of him, pushing slightly on his chest to the rhythm of Stayin' Alive.

The ambulance sped through the street lights, seemingly floating above the potholes the filled the road. In between consciousness, Henry could hear the blaring of the sirens filling his already hurting head. He didn't know how he got in the back of an ambulance or why for that matter. His mind was a blur, not recognizing where he was at times.

Darkness set over his mind as he drifted off into an unconscious state again. The paramedic looked at the monitor above Henry's head as he began to flatline. Hurriedly, he pulled out a defibrillator and gave Henry a shock in attempt to keep him alive.

- - - - -

Earlier that day - It was a cold and dreary day outside; the rain was coming down hard and the clouds hid the sun. Wanda Hare sat at her kitchen counter with her husband George, sipping their morning coffee while reading the paper.

Wanda was a former high school teacher, and her demeanor showed it with the way she spoke properly and had the ability to understand the minds of different people and help to mold them into better people. She was a small woman who held a sweet smile, but even in her mid-sixties she was able to take care of her grandsons when they needed her and to help her daughter in rough financial times. Wanda took a sip from her coffee and looked up at George. He was a southern gentleman, born and raised on a farm, constantly working shirtless in the beating heat of the sun, which his dark complexion was an everlasting reminder of. Even in his seventies, his wit was always sharp and on point.

"George," Wanda called out. George's head was still buried in the morning paper. He didn't have his hearing aids in, Wanda was going to have to speak a little louder. "George," Wanda called out again.

"Huh?" George responded, looking up from his paper.

"Have you talked to Henry lately?" Henry was Wanda and George's eldest grandson. His mom, Michelle, was their only child. Having grandchildren had been a blessing for the two, and they wanted to build memories for them that they could carry for a lifetime.

"He was 'posed to come by yesterday to go huntin' wit me an' Joe," George said in his thick country accent. "But he called an' said he had homework he had to get done."

"Has Joe said anything about Henry lately?"

"Yeah, Joe an' me went down to the farm yesterday," George said, completely mishearing his wife.

"No, George. Has Joe said anything about how Henry has been doing lately?" Wanda asked, irritated.

"Yeah, Joe seen a buck but missed. I didn't see nothin' though."

"George, put your damn hearing aids in!" Wanda bellowed. George clearly heard his wife that time, as he reached for his hearing aids sitting in the middle of the kitchen counter. "Thank you," Wanda chimed. "Now, has Joe said anything about how Henry has been doing?"

"Nu-uh, seems he's doin' pretty good. He had that big episode last year, but han't had anything else like it since. Still some moments here and there, but nothin' serious."

Wanda looked down at her coffee, lightened by creamer and sugar. Her grandson had dealt with a lot of struggles over the past year. Growing up, she had always noticed he had a tendency to lose his temper more quickly than normal, but being a high school principal it was something she was accustomed to and didn't think twice about it when it came to her grandson. It wasn't until last year that she really understood what had contributed to his mood swings for all those years.

Wanda had experienced some of Henry's angriest moments. He could be frightening. At times, she didn't recognize him. The fits of fury that would encapsulate him, the fury in his voice, his body trembling, his eyes black, his teeth grinding, it was terrifying.

Wanda looked back up from her cup of coffee as she heard George's cell phone begin to ring. "Yello," George answered.

"Hey grandpa, are you planning on going hunting tonight?" Henry asked from the other end of the phone.

"Yea, I think Joe an' me are plannin' on goin' tonight if this rain goes on somewhere."

"Alright, I think I'm going to come over after class and go with y'all tonight. If that's okay."

"Yup, come on by. We'll be here," George said as he hung up. George looked up at Wanda. "Speak o' the devil," George smiled. "Henry's plannin' on comin' by after class today."

Wanda smiled. She always loved seeing her grandson. His visits had come further and further apart since he had started college and moved away from home. They lived just across the road from his mom, so anytime he came to visit his mom, he would come to visit Wanda and George as well.

Wanda began to think back on the bond George and Henry held when he was younger. She smiled as she remembered Henry sitting in George's lap as he ran a heavy piece of equipment digging retention ponds, the smile on Henry's small face as he clapped his hands anytime George dug up another mound of dirt. She remembered him always wanting to go fishing with his grandpa, the two sitting on the bank of a pond, fishing poles in one hand and peanut butter and jelly sandwiches in the other. She thought of Henry wanting a straw hat just like George wore when he worked out in the garden, and the look on Henry's face when George would give him his to wear. Henry constantly beat himself up as he got older and would continually tell Wanda how useless and unimportant he felt in the grand scheme of the world. Henry had always been such a sweet boy growing up, and no matter what Henry thought, nothing had changed.

George looked over at his wife's delicate smile as she held her cup of coffee between her frail hands. *"She must be thinkin' 'bout Henry,"* George thought to himself. George loved both of his grandkids with everything he had, he had even retired early so that he could help Michelle take care of them as they got older. Henry had taken after his grandmother in a lot of different ways, especially the way he had excelled in grade school and now in college. He would never forget the smile on Henry's face when his grandma read his short stories. He remembered visiting his wife at work when Henry was younger and seeing him curled up underneath her desk taking a nap. He laughed when he thought of Wanda trying to potty train Henry, only to find Henry using the bathroom behind a shower curtain exclaiming 'I want privacy Granmama!'

George and Wanda both looked at each other and smiled, after fifty years of marriage they had a habit of knowing what the other was thinking. As their eyes met, they noticed the rain outside beginning to slow and the sun starting to peek through the dark clouds.

- - - - -

Henry slid his phone into his pocket and walked to his next class, Accounting 205. As he sat down in his chair, slung his bag onto his desk, and prepared for class, Henry noticed an empty airplane bottle of Patron roll out of his bag.

Henry had been drinking more the last few weeks – his anxiety had been building as finals were coming up later in the week. He couldn't help but be afraid of failing and thoughts of not graduating were not far behind. This always happened when finals came up. He normally smoked cigarettes to cope, but this semester he had turned to drinking because his anxiety had peaked with graduation coming up and he was terrified of not making it.

Henry's best friend since his first semester in college, Lisa, quickly picked up the empty bottle and handed it to Henry as she walked into class. Henry shoved it back in his bag and looked over at Lisa.

Henry had always thought she was beautiful, with her skin a radiant brown, and a smile that created a bronze glow around her. Her long dark hair covered both of her breasts, sneaking around her body. She had been one of his best friends over the last few years, but Henry had chosen not to tell her about his problems. He was afraid he would drive her away if he did, and he valued her friendship too much.

"A little early for that, isn't it?" she laughed as she pulled her notebook out of her bag and looked at Henry.

"I'm just stressed out," Henry lied.

"Henry. You are way too smart to be stressed out," she said, blinking her long eyelashes in his direction. "I wish I was half as smart as you. I would never have to worry about studying!"

As their professor walked into the room, Henry took out his binder and pencil and pushed the bag under his chair in an attempt to hide his guilty pleasure, thankful that Lisa was the only one who had seen it.

"Welcome class," the professor began. "I hope everyone remembered that we will be taking our final today and not Thursday, as I will be out of town. If you didn't remember. Oh well, be prepared to take it anyways."

A look of horror came across Henry's face. He looked over at the calm demeanor Lisa wore. Had he remembered the final was today? No. Did he study for it last night? No, he drank his sorrows away instead. He instantly began to feel sick to his stomach, and not from the alcohol.

His stomach was in knots as his mind began to race about the final. Was he prepared? Did he know the material enough to scrape by? What grade did he need on the final to pass the course? Could he get out of the final? Henry slowly put his head down on his desk, holding back an outbreak of tears.

Thinking back to how his mom told him she coped with her anxiety, Henry attempted to breathe in slow, deep breaths. As much as he wanted these breathing exercises his mom taught him to work, they rarely did. He was able to breathe better, but the constriction of his chest and the pit where his heart should be always remained.

- - - - -

Wanda sat in her rocking chair on her back porch, embracing the now sunny day. As she sat there rocking back and forth, she saw the red gleam of her grandson's Mustang coming down the dirt road. She watched Henry as he got out of his car and slammed his door shut, rather violently.

"Hey buddy!" Wanda called out across the yard to her grandson.

"Hi," Henry said in a cold, unenthusiastic tone as he walked towards his grandma on the porch.

"How was class?"

"It was awful."

"Why? What happened?"

"Had my final today," Henry scoffed. His mind was still on the test, switching from one question to another, wondering if he chose the right answers. After talking with Lisa after class about the exam, he didn't feel confident at all about this one, and the constant worrying was giving him a serious migraine. Through the pain, he closed his left eye to avoid the blaring sun, attempted to regain his blurred vision, his brow furrowed, and holding back the nausea building within him.

"How'd you do?" Wanda asked, expecting a positive answer.

"How am I supposed to know? Do you think they just grade it on the spot?" Henry snapped back.

"No Henry. I just meant how you think you did honey."

"Who knows, I probably failed. I'm sure Lisa did great, but I probably failed. And no, before you ask, Lisa is not my girlfriend. She is just a friend, so no need to pry. Where's grandpa?" Henry said, quickly changing the subject after realizing his snarky response to his grandma.

"He's in the shed honey," Wanda said, looking down at the glass of tea she held. *"Henry is truly a sweet young man, who just has a few battles he's fighting through,"* she thought to herself.

The look on Henry's face whenever he got stressed out and the way he seemed to be avoiding his family lately, she could tell he felt like he was fighting them alone, and it broke her heart that he thought that. She and George would always be there to help him. She tried to let his fits of rage roll off her shoulders, because she knew he didn't mean it. But it still hurt when he snapped like this.

- - - - -

George was standing in his shed tinkering on his tractor when he heard the crunch of rocks underneath someone's feet coming towards his shed. He sat his wrench down, dabbed his brow with an old grease rag, and lifted his Diet Pepsi can to his lips and took a swig. As the door to his shed squeaked open, letting a flood of sunlight into the dimly lit shed, he saw his grandson walk in. "Hey boy," George smiled at Henry.

"Hey grandpa," Henry replied. "What time are you planning on leaving to go to the farm?" 'The farm' was where Henry had hunted since he was a young boy. It was one hundred acres of family land that had belonged to his grandpa's family for hundreds of years. It was where his grandpa had spent most of his youth farming and tending to animals, but now they leased the land out to a farmer now, hence the name 'the farm'. It was where they hunted during deer season. Henry considered it a safe space, somewhere he could go to escape the everyday worries in life.

"Welp, I reckon we need to see when Joe will be home an' if he's plannin'a go."

"Have you talked to him today?"

"Yeahuh, talked to him 'bout an hour ago. Said he might not be home in time to go. Said he'da lemme know by four. What times it now?"

Henry pulled his phone out and glanced down at the time on the screen. "It's time for you to get a watch," Henry laughed. George reached up and gave Henry a playful slap on the back of the head, laughing as he did. "No, its 3:45 now," Henry finished.

"Alright, lemme give him a call right fast an' see if he's goin'," George said as he pulled his own phone out of his pocket. George slid the glasses from the top of his head down to his face and held the phone at arm's length. He squinted as he struggled to see the numbers on his phone's keyboard, taking his index finger and slowly poking at the numbers.

Henry chuckled to himself as his grandpa struggled to dial the number. It wasn't funny that he was struggling, but his grandpa was fulfilling the stereotypical out of touch with technology baby boomer. Henry loved his grandparents and cherished moments like this with them.

Henry broke his distant gaze as he heard his grandpa finishing up the phone call with Joe. Henry looked over at his grandpa to see what the verdict was. "Looks like Joe ain't goin' today. Said he's workin' late. So, whenever you ready, we'll load up an' go." Henry, with a smile on his face, turned around and took off to the 'man cave' where they kept their hunting supplies.

Henry's mind was now off his miserable final and was now on doing the thing that relaxed him the most. As he entered the man cave and got his camouflage gear together, Henry sat down on the couch and began sliding his boots on his feet. As he slid his shirt over his head, he got up and walked to the gun cabinet, opening it to reveal George, Joe, and Henry's collection of rifles and shotguns.

The shiny black of his Remington .270 stood out, with the brass bullet casings lining the shoulder strap. As he reached out to grab the rifle, he stopped. He stared at the top of the barrel, his eyes slowly walking down the barrel and on to the shiny silver of the trigger. *"It would be so easy..."* Henry thought to himself as he reached out and ran his fingers down the barrel. A chill went down Henry's body. He didn't know where this thought came from, but something about it felt right.

His body went numb as he began to imagine setting his chin on the barrel of the gun. He felt the cool of the metal resting against the bottom of his chin, his head bobbing upwards as he took a deep breath. He closed his eyes as he imagined his hand resting on the trigger guard. He caressed the black trigger guard, running his finger from one end to the other, and back again. His finger sliding to the silver trigger, wiggling it back and forth, feeling the play in the hair trigger. Henry took a deep breath and… opened his eyes. He shuddered. He had never had a thought like that. So real and vivid, he could feel the cold against his chin, the metal trigger beneath his fingers. It was all too real.

Henry grabbed his rifle and slung it around his shoulder as he turned to leave. Henry met his grandpa at his truck, carefully set his rifle behind the seat, wiped the dirt off his seat pretentiously, and climbed in the passenger seat. As George shifted the truck into drive and took off, Henry leaned his head against the cool window and stared at the trees and brush as they rolled by.

"Henry," George called out from the driver's seat.

"Yes grandpa?"

"You alright buddy?"

"Yeah, just thinking about some stuff. I had a final exam today and I was not ready for it at all," Henry replied with a sigh.

"Bud, you a smart youngin'. Even if you wasn't ready, I know you did just fine. You ain't even gotta worry 'bout that," George said, looking over at Henry with a smile.

For some reason, whether it was fear or respect, Henry could never get angry and yell at George. No matter how irritated he would become, he still managed to keep a cool head about him when talking to his grandpa. Maybe it was the way his grandpa said things with his southern twang, or maybe he just respected his grandpa more than anyone else. Whatever the reason, he couldn't get angry with his grandpa.

"Yeah, I guess so. I just wasn't ready for it," Henry finally said.

"Well, why wasn't ya ready?"

"I don't know, I thought it was Thursday, so I hadn't studied for it yet."

"Don't you worry 'bout it. I'm prouda you either way buddy." Henry smiled as the words came out of his grandpa's mouth. The one thing he wanted most in life was to make his family proud, and to hear his grandpa say he was proud of him made him realize he was at least on the right track.

- - - - -

Henry felt the truck go from the asphalt of the road to the bumpy terrain of the farm. He surveyed the open field to see if he could see any deer as his grandpa drove to his ladder-stand leaned against an old oak tree. As the truck came to a stop, Henry leaped out the truck, grabbed his rifle, and looked at his grandpa. "See you in an hour," he called to his grandpa with a smile as he walked to the stand.

As George drove away to his stand, Henry stepped on the bottom rung of his ladder and began to climb to the top. About three quarters of the way up the twenty-foot stand, Henry felt one of his feet slip off the rung. His chin came down and slammed against the ladder, causing Henry to cringe in pain. His grip on the side of the ladder tightened as he attempted to hold on and keep control. Once he got his foot back under control, Henry reached up and rubbed his chin.

"Damn that hurt," he thought to himself. His mind began to go back to the thought he had earlier in the day. The cold of the metal ladder against his chin sent thoughts of the cold rifle barrel pushed up into the bottom of his chin. Henry shook his head as if that might shake the thoughts out and kept climbing

Henry finally made his way to the top of the stand and got settled into his seat, rifle leaned up against the shooting rail, and slowed his breathing. As he sat there, he started to realize just how tired and exhausted he was from the night before. His eyes began to feel like they had anchors weighing them down, and every time he tried to open them it felt like a wave catching the anchor and yanking it back down. His eyes would stay closed for longer and longer each time they shut, until finally he felt himself doze off into a deep sleep.

Henry felt a breeze of cold air slap him across the face, causing him to wake up from his slumber twenty feet in the air. As he opened his eyes, he had to blink a couple of times to adjust to the new darkness that had replaced the sunlight. It had to be close to the end of legal shooting time, Henry could barely make out anything more than shadows across the field. As he sat there listening for the sound of his grandpa's truck as a signal for him to come down, he heard a rustle in the woods behind him.

"I must have timed that just right," Henry thought to himself. Henry remained as still as Death, waiting for the deer to appear from the wood line behind him. He was beginning to get impatient as he waited for the noise behind himself to reveal its identity.

He felt a sudden burst of wind across his body and a shake on his ladder-stand. Shocked, Henry looked down underneath him to see what had shaken his stand. It was too dark to tell what it was, but it almost looked like the outline of a person standing underneath him. A chill ran down Henry's spine as the person grabbed onto his stand and began to climb up.

"HEY!" Henry yelled out. "There's someone up here!" His bellows didn't seem to deter the person climbing the stand. He looked up to make sure his rifle was near enough for him to grab. To his astonishment, his rifle was gone. He glanced down and saw a sliver of silver from underneath his stand. *"Must have fell when the stand shook,"* Henry thought to himself.

"I'm coming," a voice bellowed from below.

As the figure got closer and closer, Henry still couldn't make out any of its features. The figure reminded him of the one from his reoccurring dreams. He began looking around to see if he could see his grandpa's truck or find a loose limb on the tree to use as a weapon, but he found nothing. He felt a hand grab onto his ankle and sharp objects digging into the skin surrounding his ankle. Henry screamed out in pain as what felt like screws began to sink deeper and deeper into his ankle. With his free foot, Henry kicked down towards the figure to try and get him off.

Henry's boot cracked against the bottom of the ladder-stand, connecting with the metal and causing a loud *CLANK*. Henry's eyes shot open, finding himself surrounded by the light of a slowly falling sun, his rifle still sitting across from him, and nobody underneath him. *"I haven't had that dream in a while,"* he thought to himself as he reached down and rubbed his sore ankle. Even though he knew the attacker wasn't real, the pain pulsed through his body.

As Henry sat there rubbing his ankle, something caught his eye across the field. He squinted his eyes, trying to get a better look at what was there. *"This better not be another damn dream."* Henry thought to himself. As he slowly reached over to grab his rifle, he caught a glimmer of white off the object. *"That's a damn deer!"* He slowly and carefully grabbed his rifle, moving at the speed of a snail and attempting to not make a single noise. He knew he had to be extremely quiet and slow with his movement in order to not scare the deer away.

The deer took a few steps away from the wood line and into the field, leaning down to eat off the beans planted in the field. Henry took this opportunity to slowly lift his rifle and rest it gently on the shooting rail. The deer was in a perfect broadsided position. Henry rested his cheek against the stock of the rifle and closed one eye, looking through the scope with his other. It was getting darker by the second and harder for Henry to try and find the deer through the scope.

Henry slowly and gently drifted the rifle around the field, looking through the scope, to try and get the deer in his crosshairs. The deer's head shot up and looked in Henry's direction. Henry got as still as he could, waiting for the deer to look away. It was perfectly in his crosshairs now and Henry could clearly count twelve tall tines on his antlers. Its eyes were uncharacteristically sky-blue.

The deer looked back down to eat and Henry took this as his opportunity. Henry took a deep breath and held it to steady himself. He slowly wrapped his finger around the trigger of his rifle, pulling it ever so slowly. *CRACK*. Henry heard the crack of the gunshot and saw a quick burst of fire out the end of the rifle. The gunshot shattered the air around him. The bullet tore through the empty space and silence of the forest. Henry rechambered another bullet as he looked up to see if the deer had fallen.

Henry saw the deer get low to the ground, and he thought he had hit him. Then, the deer, still low to the ground, took off running to the wood line like a bat out of Hell. Henry looked back through the scope, trying to lead the deer by a hair, and fired a pop shot. Henry went to rechamber another bullet as he saw the deer disappear into the woods. *"Oh, you have got to be kidding me,"* Henry thought to himself as he prepared to climb down the ladder. He hoped he had hit it, and he thought he would have to track the deer through the woods.

As Henry hurried down the ladder, both feet missed one of the ladder's rungs and Henry slid the remainder of the ten feet down the ladder. As Henry slid down, he clobbered his chin on the remaining rungs of the ladder and landed on his back, his rifle lying next to him. Henry laid there for a minute, trying to recover from his fall. His whole body was sore, his head hurt, but he forced himself off the ground to go track the deer.

Henry pulled his cellphone out of his coat pocket and called his grandpa. "Did you hit 'em?" his grandpa asked, sparing no time for pleasantries, as he answered the phone.

"I don't know, I think so. I thought I saw him drop the first shot," Henry said, out of breath as he made his way through the sea of beanstalks.

"Alright, Ima be there in a sec to help ya track 'em down."

Henry hung up and switched his phone into flashlight mode as he made his way across the field. He stopped every few feet to turn and see if he could line himself up with his ladder-stand, trying to get a more precise location of where he thought the deer was when he shot at him. He continued to trudge through the beanstalks, the stalks slowing him down every step like the current of the ocean catching his feet. He finally came across a pile of churned up dirt, appearing to be where the deer had run. He began shining his light at the ground, attempting to find droplets of blood to begin tracking the deer with.

"There has to be some blood around here somewhere," Henry thought to himself as he searched the ground with his eyes and light. He heard the crunch of beanstalks underneath heavy weight as his grandpa's truck made its way towards

him. He knew that if there was blood, his grandpa would be able to find it.

"You see any sign yet?" George asked as he got out of the truck.

"I found running tracks right here," Henry said as he shined the light on the churned up dirt. "But I can't find any blood. There has to be some around here somewhere."

"Ya sure you hit 'em?"

"Pretty sure. I saw him drop to the ground."

"Mkay, lemme take a looks 'round here," George said as he pulled out his flashlight. George shined the light on the churned up dirt and looked at it for about thirty seconds. Then, like some spirit took over his body, his head made a quick jerk to the left and he began walking in a perfect line without saying anything. George was following the tracks towards the woods, finding no blood from the field to the wood line.

"Do you see anything?" Henry called out.

Without saying a word, George turned and followed his exact path back to the initial track, his eyes never leaving the ground and continuing to search. His head surveying the untouched ground around the track, trying to find some indication. "There," George said, pointing at the ground a few feet from the track Henry had found.

Henry, excited at the thought his grandpa had found blood, ran to where his grandpa was pointing. However, Henry didn't see any blood, all he saw was a large mound of dirt. "Here what?"

"That right there," George said, wetting his lips. "Is where the bullet hit the ground. 'Fraid ya missed 'em bud."

"No, that can't be," Henry said, quivering either in sadness or disappointment that he had missed. "I saw him fall."

"Sometimes, them deer will drop on down low like 'at to take off runnin'."

Henry felt defeated and disappointed. He turned and drudgingly walked towards his grandpa's truck without a word. Henry slung the door open, carelessly threw his rifle in the back, and slumped into the passenger seat with mud dripping off his boots. He slammed the door shut behind him and pulled his blaze orange cap over his face.

George looked over as Henry slammed the door of his truck closed. He put his head down as he walked to the truck, feeling guilty that his grandson was upset. He knew Henry was feeling disappointed, and it hurt him to know that he was so upset. As he opened the door of the truck, the light from the dome flooding inside, he looked over at Henry slumped in his seat, hat covering his face, and arms crossed.

George climbed into the truck and shifted it into drive, leaving the bumpy terrain of the field and making his way to the smooth path of the asphalt.

- - - - -

Henry put his head against the cold of the window in his grandpa's truck, feeling his blood boiling within himself. He was past being disappointed and upset and was now at the point of being angry at himself. *"I should have hit that deer,"* Henry thought to himself. *"There is NO excuse for missing him. Maybe I should have waited for him to get closer. I shouldn't have fallen asleep. It's probably the stupid scope on that thing."*

"Henry," George called out from the driver's side of the truck, cutting off Henry's train of thought.

"Yeah," Henry replied.

"You okay bud?"

"No, I shouldn't have missed."

"Boy, you know how many of 'em deer I missed in my time? If I hada dollar for every time I missed, I'd be rich," George laughed.

"Yeah, but how many have you hit? More than me. You can actually hit them- I can't," Henry retorted.

"Well, I been huntin' a lot longer than you has too. Don't let it getcha down bud, we all miss 'em."

Henry remained silent. He didn't want to talk about it anymore, he felt himself getting angrier. He knew his grandpa meant well, but it didn't help the way he felt.

- - - - -

Wanda saw the lights of her husband's truck shine through the blinds of her window. She got up from her chair and poured two glasses of tea. She walked to the door, staring out as the men pulled up and got out of the truck. She opened the door and made her way to the truck to bring them tea and see if they had tagged a deer.

"You guys get anything?" Wanda asked, sitting the tea down on the bed of the truck. George shot a look towards her, indicating something was wrong with Henry.

"Nope, I missed," Henry snapped. "Of course, that's pretty much how my life goes. I shoot. I miss. I'm no good at anything I actually enjoy." He felt his blood boiling up again, his body getting hot, and his ears tingling.

"It's okay buddy, there's always next time," Wanda said to Henry, reaching out and lightly touching his arm to try and encourage him.

"No. No there's not," Henry once again snapped, snatching his hat off his head and slinging it to the ground.

"What do you mean buddy?" Wanda asked, looking over at George who also had a confused look on his face.

"I'm selling my rifle. I'm selling my tree stand. I'm selling my hunting boots. I quit, I'm done being a failure at everything!" Henry yelled, his eyes twitching and looking over at his grandmother. Wanda looked into Henry's eyes, watching as his pupils grew. She could always tell when he was on the verge of an outburst.

"I'm just done!" Henry yelled, slamming his fist on the toolbox of the truck. He put his head where he had just slammed his fist and bellowed into the metal of the toolbox, "Everything I love to do, everything I want to do, I can't do. I'm so over it! I'm better off dead!"

Henry's body was now shaking, his eyes looked like the night sky as his pupils had finished covering the rest of its surrounding. Wanda and George could hear the sound of his teeth grinding together, echoing within his mouth like nails on a chalkboard. "Why am I so useless!" he yelled as he looked up at the sky.

Wanda and George began to get frightened. They hadn't seen him this angry in a long time. It was like a demon had possessed Henry's body and was wreaking havoc from within. George reached out to put his hand on Henry's shoulder to try and calm him down.

"Don't touch me!" Henry yelled, his mind afraid of what he might do. He jerked his body away, slamming into the side of his grandpa's truck. Henry had just yelled at his grandpa for the first time, and it made him even angrier at himself.

"Henry, please calm down honey," Wanda pleaded, as she felt the tears forming beneath her eyes.

"YOU CALM DOWN," Henry shouted as he reached out to grab the glass of tea. Shaking and trembling, he lifted the glass to his mouth and clanked it against his teeth while trying to take a drink. The pain of the hardened glass smacking his teeth sent chills through his body.

"FUCK!" Henry yelled, slamming the glass down on the ground beneath him. His frustration had built within himself, and he was now feeling even more useless. The glass shattered into a thousand different pieces, as Henry felt like his reflection looked back at him in each piece disapprovingly, trying to tell him he was making a mistake. But there was no turning back now. "I can't even fucking drink tea!"

"Hey!" George yelled out, now fearing for his wife's safety from their own grandson. "You don't talk like that 'round yer grandma. And don't be slammin' stuff 'round here!"

Henry didn't hear anything his grandparents were saying; his body was overwhelmed with anger. All he could hear was his heart pounding within his chest like the beat of a piston deep within an engine.

His body felt like it was on fire, every bone and organ burning with the fury of rage. He started to sweat profusely. His breathing intensified as his chest tightened from the fiery rage building within. The world began to turn around him.

"I CAN'T FUCKING DO IT ANYMORE!" he yelled as he took off for his car.

"Henry!" Wanda called out.

"Buddy, come on," George pleaded.

Henry couldn't hear his grandparents' pleas. He got in his car and cranked it up. He couldn't make out the sound of his engine roaring through the sound of his heart pounding within his chest. All he knew was that he wanted to get away from his current surroundings. He wanted the Earth to stop spinning. He slammed his car into reverse as he backed out of his grandparent's driveway.

As he looked behind him, he couldn't help to notice the mound of trash and dirt that had been building up in his back seat. The mess infuriated him even more. Without waiting for the car to come to a complete stop, Henry slammed the gear shifter into drive as he felt the abrupt jump of the transmission shifting.

- - - - -

Wanda looked over at George, who had his head down, and asked him, "George, is he going to be okay?"

"I dunno. I ain't ever seen him this mad 'fore," George said as he kicked the rocks and glass beneath his feet, trying to get the glass away from his wife and his truck's tires.

Wanda looked over at the cloud of dust her grandson was leaving behind as he traveled down the dirt road. Her vision was blurred as the tears welled up in her eyes. She saw the car coming up on the sharp curve, where he would disappear out of sight.

Wanda, however, noticed Henry wasn't slowing down as he got closer and closer to the curve. *"Henry please,"* she thought to herself as she brought her hands together and up to her face.

- - - - -

Henry felt his body trembling as he traveled down the dirt road. He was so angry, he couldn't focus on the road. He glanced down at his speedometer, noticing he was going 70 mph down a road where the speed limit was 35 mph. He looked back up and realized he was coming up on the curve taking him to the main road. He had to make a decision: Try to make the curve at the speed he was going or attempt to slow down on the muddy road.

Henry made the decision to keep his speed and try to make the turn. As he came around the corner, he felt the back of the car begin to slide away from him. *"Shit,"* Henry thought to himself as he grabbed the steering wheel. Henry spun the steering wheel of the car in a panic, over correcting the car and sending him into a spiral.

- - - - -

George looked up from the ground as he heard the sickening groans of metal being twisted and warped. He saw a cloud of dust and smoke forming near the curve down the road.

"Henry," George heard his wife whimper.

George leaped into action, jumping into his truck and taking off towards the clouds of dust. The remaining glass slung off the back of the truck and spiraled to the ground as he sped off towards his grandson. He looked in his rearview mirror to see his wife, with her face buried in her hands. George turned his attention back to the cloud of dust and smoke in the distance, as he hurried down the dirt road.

"Henry, Henry, Henry. Why buddy," George whispered to himself as he approached the wreckage. As he got closer, he could make out Henry's car on its side in the middle of the curve. He slowed down as he approached the car turned on its side and got out of the truck. George stared at the car in fear as he pulled his phone out to call 911.

- - - - -

Henry shot awake, gasping for air as he looked around him. He didn't know where he was. It was a small, white room. His body was sore, his limbs were stiff, and there was a pounding in his head. He looked down and saw his arm in a cast. There were IV's running into his veins pumping him full of fluids. He knew then that he was in the hospital.

Henry heard the creak of the door slowly opening, his grandma poking her head around the door like a turtle over a log. "Oh, you're up buddy. I didn't wake you, did I?" she asked quietly.

Henry shook his head no, and asked "What happened?"

"You lost control of your car around a corner and flipped the car," Wanda said, holding in tears as she thought back to the sight of the first responders pulling Henry's bloodied body out of the flipped car.

"What? Where?" Henry asked, looking around the hospital room.

"Leaving our house," Wanda stammered. As she finished, she heard George come in and put his hand on her shoulder.

Henry's mind flashed to the image of scissors slicing through his clothes while he laid on an operating table. His clothes were already cut and shredded, whether from the wreck or from getting them off for surgery. He remembered now, as he looked down, what happened.

As he came around the corner, Henry felt the back of the car begin to slide away from him towards the right side of the road. He gripped the steering wheel with the might of Hercules. Henry attempted to correct the car from its slide, spinning the steering wheel to the right. Henry felt he had oversteered the car and sent it into a full spin.

As the car began to lose control, Henry attempted to turn the steering wheel to the left and regain his control over the vehicle. As he felt the vehicle straightening out, Henry attempted to accelerate to give the car control.

He felt a bump as he hit a hole in the road and felt the car come off the ground. He grabbed onto the steering wheel and leaned back in his seat, bracing for impact as he felt the car tipping over. He heard the crackling of glass and felt the sparkling shards meeting his face. He felt his head jerk forward, plowing into the steering wheel.

As the car came to a halt, which Henry could only imagine was on its side because of the way his body was hanging, there was a moment of silence. It was so silent it reminded Henry of a blanket of whiteness surrounding the car. Slowly, he began to hear the sound of the blood pumping in his veins, the ***drip, drip, drip*** of fuel leaking out the car, the hissing of the radiator blowing out steam. He began to smell the dull smell of gasoline as it leaked onto ground. Dust infiltrated his nasal cavity. What smelled like iron excreted from his pores.

Henry heard the sound of a vehicle pull up near him and attempted to yell out for help. His chest hurt too bad to move or try to yell, he just hoped whoever was there would know he was in the car.

He could hear his grandpa, on the phone with 911, trying to get help. Through the pain, the terrifying sounds, the encapsulating smells, and the tastes of misery, Henry could feel the regret in his heart more than anything. How he had talked to his grandparents, how he let his blind anger take ahold of his body, had put him in this position.

What felt like hours later, the blaring sound of sirens pierced his eardrums. He could see the flashing of blue and red bouncing off the shattered glass near his face. As he attempted to turn his head, he felt a sharp pain shoot down his neck. He remained still as he heard the metal of the door being peeled off his car.

The smell of fuel, dust, and iron began to flow out of his nostrils. The sound of the fuel dripping, the sirens, the hissing of the radiator slowly floated away from his ears. The blue and red of the sirens, the ember flames crackling in front of him began to escape his eyes. His world was fading away as he laid there in pain.

Henry felt like he was truly dying.

That was all Henry could vividly remember from the accident. His memory of being pulled out of the car, being put in the ambulance, the ride to the hospital, and the surgery he underwent were all broken fragments.

"You okay?" George asked Henry, noticing he had been looking down at his chest for some time now.

Henry looked up and glanced over at his grandparents. His fit of rage had caused his accident. He knew he had hurt them. He thought about the glass shattering on the ground and the look of his reflections. He thought about the fear overcoming his grandmother's face as his rage grew. He thought about the newfound mixture of anger, fear, and disappointment in his grandpa's voice.

"I'm sorry," Henry cried. He knew he had hurt them, and he regretted it. The tears flowed from his face like the blood had flowed from his nose. He looked down at his chest again, watching as the tears beat against it.

"Henry," Wanda said, running to her grandson and wrapping her arms around him carefully. George followed her to Henry's bedside and kneeled beside them.

"I'm so sorry," Henry said again. He didn't know what else to say.

"Bud, it's okay," George said, grabbing his grandson's hand and gripping it tight.

Henry felt his grandpa's tough as rock hands, scattered with rough spots from calluses he had earned over his years of working in a field. He felt the wrinkles covering his grandpa's hand like waves on the ocean. While his grandpa held a tough exterior, his hands were cool to the touch as he held Henry.

"I don't know what came over me," Henry started. "I'm sorry. I'm sorry for how I acted and what I did and what I said. I didn't mean any of it," Henry said in between gasps of air and sobs. "I hurt y'all. I never want to hurt y'all again. I love y'all."

Michelle, Joe, and Leonard walked into Henry's hospital room, seeing a beautiful sight in an otherwise unsettling setting. Michelle put her hand on Joe's chest and rested her head against him, while Joe wrapped his arm around her. Leonard looked at his brother, wrapped in white rags, with a look of despair in his eyes. Henry was sobbing into his grandmother's shoulder, while she held him like she did when he was born. His grandpa looked over both of them, like a majestic buck looking over its herd and making sure no harm came their way.

"I won't ever treat you like that again," Henry promised his grandparents.

PART 3:
LEONARD HOVISHKY
THREE YEARS AGO

- - - - -

Henry sat in the dark and ominous waiting room of the hospital, waiting for his brother Leonard to get out of surgery. The waiting room was small, much smaller than what Henry would have expected from a hospital this large, the lights overhead were dim, and the room smelled of sickness. He glanced over at an elderly couple sitting a few seats down from him. The wife, probably in her late sixties, sat in her chair mindlessly flipping through the pages of a magazine. The husband, a few years older than his wife, had his chin to his chest and was faintly snoring as he struggled to stay awake. Henry chuckled to himself. They reminded him of his grandparents. The last time he was in the hospital, other people were waiting to see him. It was the accident he had last year after a bipolar episode caused one of his worst meltdowns ever.

Henry shivered as the thoughts from the accident swarmed back into his head. The flashing of the lights from the ambulance, the panic in his grandfather's voice, the smell of gasoline, the taste of iron in his mouth. He reached up and rubbed the scar on his head from the accident.

"Michelle West?" A voice called out from the door into the waiting room. Michelle and Joe stood up to go to meet the nurse.

Michelle stopped when they got to the nurse and turned back to look at Henry. "Are you coming honey?" Michelle asked him. Joe, with his hands on Michelle's small shoulders, turned and looked at Henry looking down at the floor gazing distantly.

"You okay bud?" Joe asked.

"Yeah, sorry. Just got caught up daydreaming," Henry laughed as he got up. As he approached his mom and Joe, he turned and gave one last look at the elderly couple in the waiting room. A smile crept across his face as he thought about how his grandparents had always supported him and Leonard. The support they showed Henry, despite his angry outburst and frightening actions, after his accident last year demonstrated how they always treated them. No matter how Henry or Leonard acted, whether they were arguing with each other or having a bad day, their grandparents always showed them love and support.

Henry turned around to follow his mom, Joe, and the nurse back to his brother's hospital recovery room. His brother, Leonard, was four years younger than him at 18 years old and had enjoyed a successful baseball career in high school. He had received several college offers by his junior year.

However, his baseball career was derailed. After years of overuse, he tore his shoulder labrum his senior year when he threw his first pitch of the season. Henry remembered seeing his brother grimace and grab his shoulder after he had thrown the pitch, falling to his knees in pain. He went from a three-year average of 63 innings pitched, 1.02 ERA, and 78 strikeouts to his worst season his senior year of 48 innings pitched, 6.74 ERA, and 20 strikeouts. After the season, he found out he had a torn labrum throughout the season and lost all his college offers.

Henry partially blamed their blood father for his brother's misfortune. His blood father had pushed his brother to pitch and play baseball year-round with no breaks. It turned out that the only break Leonard would have, would be his labrum. It made Henry angry just thinking about what their blood father did to his brother. As the anger came over him, he looked up at Joe, holding onto his mom's hand tightly, and calmed down. He was glad his mom had met Joe. He had proven to be a real father to him and Leonard.

The nurse took a sharp left down a long hallway. Henry looked up at the lights on the ceiling, flashing with every step he took. The light at the end of the hallway was flickering on and off, and Henry fixated his gaze on that light as he walked. He felt like he was in a hospital show on TV. The light almost blinded Henry as he fixated on the blinking bulb.

WHAM!

Henry ran right into the door at the end of the hallway. *"Watch out for that wall Henry,"* He thought to himself as he reached up to rub his forehead and turned around to see if anyone had seen him run into the wall, and sure enough his mom and Joe, and all of the nurses working the hallway, were staring at him.

"Well son," Michelle started, holding back a giggle.

"I got way too focused on this light," Henry said as he pointed above his head at the blinking light.

"Yes, maintenance is supposed to be coming to fix it," the nurse said, rubbing her chin and staring at the light.

"Not just the light bulb," Henry started, looking back down at the nurse. "If you look at the light and line it up with the others, it doesn't match. It's slightly further left."

"Huh," the nurse said, perplexed, as she looked up and ran her eyes down the line of lights. "I never noticed that before."

"Henry definitely has a keen eye," Joe chuckled, half amazed that Henry had noticed such a small error and half laughing at Henry running into the wall. "Is this Leonard's room?" Joe asked the nurse, turning to the room nearest to them.

"Yes, sorry," she responded as she reached for the door handle. "He's probably going to be a little loopy right now. We gave him morphine when he woke up to help with the pain. The doctor will be in shortly to talk to y'all," she said as she opened the door to Leonard's room and held it open for the family.

"Well hello there fam," Leonard called in a slurred voice from his hospital bed.

"Hey buddy," Michelle responded, trying not to laugh.

"Sup? What'cha up to mane?" Leonard called back, smiling a creepy grin and looking over at Henry.

"Man, they have you on that good, good, don't they?" Henry laughed.

"DAAAAYUM straight they do!"

"Leonard!" Michelle called out.

"Sorry ma, I'm still stuck in my Cancun days. Selling drugs and gettin' bitches," Leonard called back to her, with his eyes almost shut.

"LEONARD!" she called again. Before Michelle could begin scolding Leonard, there was a soft knock at the door as the doctor came into the room.

"Hello everyone. Hello Leonard," The doctor- an older man in his fifties, with a slim build, a scraggly head of grey hair, a sincere smile, and wise eyes that highlighted his honest disposition- said as he smiled and looked around the room. "The good news: Leonard's surgery went successfully. As you know, the labral tear extended down into Leonard's bicep tendons. We were able to repair the labral tear and reattach the tendon with sutures. Leonard, you will need to wear a sling for about three to four weeks while you recover. You must be VERY careful during the first few weeks, the chance for those sutures ripping is high in the beginning."

"Yo, when can I go play baseball again doc?" Leonard said, as his head flopped down to his chest.

"Well, that's the bad news. I highly recommend you wait three to four months before going back to any baseball related activities. We will put you on physical therapy next month as long as the healing process is going well. You will need to go to some specialized PT for about two to three months. Even then though, the comeback rate for baseball pitchers after this surgery is extremely low, as the labral is more likely to tear again. I'm not trying to be negative, but we need to set a realistic expectation."

Henry felt his fists clenching as the doctor said his brother may not be able to pitch again. He knew his brother wanted to try to walk onto a college baseball team, and his chances seemed slim to none now. *"Damn you, dad,"* Henry thought to himself.

"What should we give him for pain? Advil, Tylenol?" Michelle asked the doctor.

"I'm prescribing him Oxycodone for pain. Just be careful with it, though, they will be 5 mg tablets."

"Awww yeah boi. Gonna be flyin' high like a plane," Leonard said as he slowly nodded his head and waved his hand in the air like it was an airplane.

"LEONARD, stop it!" Michelle said, this time trying to hold back a laugh.

- - - - -

Henry pulled back into the driveway of his apartment and parked his Mustang in his designated spot. Henry's insurance company had declared his car totaled after his wreck, so he took the money and bought the car back and repaired it. He loved this car.

Henry looked down as his phone dinged with the sound of an incoming text. *[Thank u for coming to the hospital with us today buddy]* the message from his mom read.

[No problem. How is Leo doing?]

[Sleeping. Do u mind picking up his prescription and bringing it by tomorrow?]

[Sure thing. Family Pharm?]

[Yes. Thank you! Love u!!! ♥♥♥]

Henry took in a deep breath and cranked his car back up, bringing the roar of the engine to life as he gripped the steering wheel and stared out aimlessly in front of him. The sound of the engine roaring would occasionally ring in Henry's ears as he would recant the accident.

Henry shook his head as if that would shake the thoughts out- something he found himself doing a lot more nowadays- and put the car into drive, leaving the apartment complex behind.

- - - - -

Henry pulled up to the pharmacy, got out of his car, and looked up at the sun shining above his head. The bright day was ironic because he had spent almost his entire day in a poorly lit and somber hospital.

As he made his way to the pharmacy counter in the back of the store, Henry's eyes scanned the aisles for any good deals. He was a bargain hunter, a trait he had picked up from his mom and grandma.

About halfway through the store, Henry stopped. There was a flashing light above the pharmacy that caught his eye. It was eerily similar to the one in the hospital that had caused him to run into the wall. And just like the hospital light, this one was also slightly out of line with the rest of the lights in its row. *"What are the chances?"* Henry thought to himself as he chuckled and continued to the pharmacy counter, more careful this time so he didn't run into something again.

Henry, his eyes still locked onto the light, thought about who would have put the lights in like that. The little things aggravated him if they were out of order. He had cleaned, rearranged, and straightened up his entire apartment last week. The lights, seemed to be taunting him, their flashes laughing in his face as he approached.

As he approached the pharmacy counter, a young purple-haired pharmacy assistant with forest green eyes and a tiny and cautious face met Henry with a smile. "What can I help you with?" She beamed.

"Uh, I'm here to pick up for Leonard Hovishky," Henry murmured, his attention still caught on the flashing light above.

"Okay. Date of birth, please?"

"June 13th, 1997."

"Okay, here it is," she said as she pulled a white bag out of a container under the counter. "Any questions for the pharmacist?"

"Uh, no. I don't think so." Henry said as he fumbled to pull his wallet out of his back pocket. "How much is it?" Henry asked, eyes still stuck on the light above.

"I'm sorry, I know the light is bothering everyone," the pharmacist assistant apologized. "The manager was supposed to fix it today. Your total comes to $3.46."

"It's also out of line with the rest of the lights," Henry said almost matter-of-factly. Henry pulled out a crumpled up five-dollar bill and handed it to the girl. She looked up at the light, inquisitively, after Henry had pointed out that it was out of line.

"Now, I'm going to be staring at that all day!" she laughed as she gave him his change.

Henry quickly left the counter. *"I have to get away from this light. I'm going to go nuts staring at it."*

Henry walked out of the pharmacy to find that it had begun to rain hard outside. The sound of the rain beating on the pavement sounded like dogs and cats running around at the pound. The constant pitter-patter of their tiny paws hitting the concrete, with occasional scrapes of their nails.

He popped the back of his shirt over his head and took off running to his car. When he was about three steps from his car, Henry slipped in a water puddle, plummeting towards the ground, and sent his brother's prescription across the parking lot. He quickly pulled himself off the ground and ran after the pill bottle floating in the stream of rainwater like a boat at sea towards a storm drain. Henry reached out as he dove forward and grabbed the bottle just as it approached the grates of the storm drain. *"You klutz,"*

Henry thought to himself, lifting himself off the ground once again.

As he opened the door of his car and slid into the driver's seat, he noticed that the lid of the pill bottle had come off when he picked it up and put it in his pocket. *"Shit, how many were supposed to be in there?"* Henry thought to himself. As he read the label, he saw the prescription was for fifteen tablets. He pulled the tablets out of his pocket and poured the ones in the pill bottle into his hand and began counting. *"Shit, I lost some. There's only ten!"* Henry thought to himself, panicked.

Henry pulled his phone out of his pocket and called his mom.

"Hey sweetie," Michelle said from the other side of the phone.

"Mom, I'm sorry," Henry started.

"What's wrong Henry?" Michelle's mind instantly went back to the night Henry had his panic attack and all he could say was sorry. Her heart dropped as she waited for her son to respond.

"It was raining when I came out the pharmacy, and I was trying to run to the car and I slipped," Henry told her panicked. "The bottle came out of my hand and the lid came off. Some of the medicine got lost. I'm so sorry."

"Henry, it's okay honey. I doubt your brother needs all of them anyways. And if he does, we can just call in another prescription. How many refills did they give him?"

Henry hadn't even thought about refills. He looked down at the bottle and found how many refills it had listed on it. "It looks like five."

"See, it'll be okay. Are you okay?"

"Yeah, why?" Henry asked, wondering why his mom was asking him that.

"Well you said you slipped. Did you get hurt?"

"Oh! No, I'm fine," Henry said, reaching down to rub his sore knee, covered with the damp denim of his jeans.

"Okay sweetie, thank you again for picking those up. Be careful driving home, I'll see you tomorrow. Love you!"

His mom had such a caring attitude about her, and Henry loved it. She made him feel comfortable and safe. "Thanks Mom, I love you too!" He hung up the phone.

As Henry pushed his phone back into his pocket, he felt his phone push down on something. Digging further into his pocket, Henry pulled out the five missing Oxycodone he thought he had lost in the rain. *"I've never taken an Oxy before,"* he thought to himself. *"I wonder if they'll help."*

- - - - -

Henry pulled onto the dirt road to his mom's house. The road, littered with potholes and muddied from the two weeks of straight rain, was always rough on his car. He got a lump in his throat every time he came around the curve where he wrecked his car. As he slowly and cautiously made his way around the curve, he could see his mom and grandparents' houses in the distance.

Henry noticed his grandmother in the distance doing yard work in her front yard. He spotted his grandfather sitting under the covering of his 'man cave' with a Bud Light in his hand. He could see his mom leaning against the railing of her front porch smoking a cigarette. A smile crept across Henry's face as nothing had changed at home. It was a picture-perfect depiction that captured his childhood memories.

As he pulled into the driveway and got out of his car, he saw Leonard walking down the steps of the back porch and approaching Henry. "Did you get my refill buddy?" Leonard asked as Henry exited the car.

"Sure did! You only have two more refills left."

"It doesn't feel like I'm using them that fast," Leonard said, in a partially puzzled tone.

"Well you probably don't remember taking them half the time!" Henry joked with his brother, his eyes glancing down at his feet and a lump forming in his throat.

"Yeah I guess so," Leonard responded.

"How are you doing man?"

"I'm getting better. Only about a week left with this sling. I've even been driving some."

"Good," Henry mumbled as he saw his mom coming down the steps of the front porch. Did she know? Was she upset? Was she going to scold him? Henry's mind raced in a thousand directions.

"Hey Henry," Michelle called out as she approached the two boys.

"Hey Mom. Where's Joe?" Henry asked, noticing Joe's truck was missing from the driveway.

"Oh, he and Johnny went to run dogs today," she said, rolling her eyes.

Before Henry could respond, his grandmother walked over to the crowd with a beaming smile and said "Hey y'all."

"Hey Granmama," Henry and Leonard said in unison.

"What're you boys up to today?" Wanda asked.

"Oh nothing, I think I'm going to go see Tracy later on. I've gotten pretty used to driving with this thing," Leonard answered, pointing at his sling.

"I just came to drop off Leo's refill. I'm probably just going to relax today," Henry replied. "it has ben a crazy and exhausting week."

"Y'all look!" Wanda called out, interrupting the conversation at hand, and pointing to the woods behind the group. As they all turned around, Henry caught the glimpse of a deer running off into the woods. After a few steps, the deer stopped and looked back at Henry, with a set of sky-blue eyes.

"Is that the same deer I shot at before my accident?" Henry thought to himself, still gazing into the woods as the rest of his family turned back around. Henry couldn't help but to be captivated by the deer. As the sky-blue eyes danced around in his mind, his body shivered at the thought of that night,

and at the oddity of the same deer appearing before him a year later.

"Leo be careful driving down there," Wanda called out, breaking Henry's distant gaze. "Don't take any of that medicine and drive!"

"I know, I know," Leonard responded, rolling his eyes and laughing.

"I'm going to mow in a bit mom," Michelle told Wanda.

It was just the way he remembered Saturdays: Leonard going to see his girlfriend, Michelle mowing the grass, Joe out hunting, Wanda doing work in her flower beds, and George sipping on his beer in the man cave. This was his family.

- - - - -

Henry pulled back into his parking spot in his apartment complex and turned the ignition off. He reached in his pocket and pulled out the three Oxycodone he had snagged from his brother's bottle.

After he found the five pills in his pocket outside the pharmacy, Henry had begun snagging a few out of his brother's bottle when he picked up the medicine. It was a way for him to relax when things got overwhelming.

Henry walked back into his apartment and headed straight for the living room to find something on TV, so he could take a quick power nap. Henry had to have background noise and the sound of a fan to sleep, he had needed that since he was a kid.

As he flipped through the channels, he landed on *Bambi* and he soon felt himself drifting off into a nice slumber. He let the sandman come in and put him to sleep for a while.

- - - - -

Henry awoke to a knock at his door. Groggy from his deep sleep, he walked to the door and looked through the peephole. It was a man who appeared to be in his mid-thirties, with a buzzed head and patchy facial hair. A strangeness emitted from him that Henry couldn't put his finger on.

He cracked the door, with the safety lock still in place as a precaution. "Yes?" Henry asked the man.

"Hey man, my van ran out of gas and my girlfriend is pregnant. She's going into labor and is about thirty miles from here. Can I get like twenty bucks for gas so I can go get her?"

Henry felt a little uneasy about the man and wasn't buying the story he was trying to sell. He had read stories on Facebook about people doing this and either taking the money and running or trying to scout out the house. Despite this, Henry's heart and conscious wouldn't let him shut the door on the man, with the thought that he really could have a pregnant girlfriend going into labor.

"Yeah, hold on and I'll be right back," Henry responded as he closed the door and walked to his room.

Henry fumbled through his wallet to get a crisp twenty dollar bill out and returned to the door. With the safety latch still in place, he opened the door and slid the twenty in between the door and door frame. "Here you go man," Henry said.

The man hurriedly grabbed the money and said a quick thank you as he ran down the flight of stairs. *"Strange,"* Henry thought to himself.

Henry closed the door and stood there for a minute. The man was awfully strange, and the fact that he now knew Henry had money frightened him. *"What if he comes back to rob me?"* he thought to himself. He shook his head and let the thoughts roll out of his mind.

Henry walked back into the living room and sank back on the couch. He reached into his pockets and felt the three pills still sitting there. *"I've taken one before, I'll probably be okay taking all three of these,"* Henry thought as he pulled all three out of his pocket. He stared down at the round, white tablets he held in his hand.

"It has been a stressful week. I just started my new job, and its only part-time. I'm grateful for having a job, but what if I never move into a full-time role? I can't afford to live off part-time. And the money really isn't that good," He thought to himself as he felt anxiety creeping through his veins and into his brain. *"I should have done more in college so I wouldn't be in this position. Lisa is out working full-time for a financial analyst and I'm here working as a part-timer. I really messed up in college…"*

As the thoughts filled his brain and the anxiety overwhelmed him, he threw his hand up to his mouth and swallowed all three pills. *"This isn't bad,"* Henry thought to himself after a few minutes. He closed his eyes and laid his head on the back of the couch, enjoying the feeling of the pills kicking in.

Henry opened his eyes to reveal a flashing light above him on his ceiling. *"I never even knew I had a light here,"* Henry said perplexed. Henry blinked a few times to clear his vision, thinking the flashing light was an illusion. After he blinked a few times and rubbed his eyes, he saw the flashing light above him had disappeared.

There was another knock at the door. *"Was twenty dollars not enough for 'gas'?"* Henry thought to himself as he got up to answer the door once again. He felt a set of chills shoot from his head to his toes as he began to think about the mysterious man again.

As he got to the door, he glanced through the peephole. There was nobody at the door. *"Damn kids,"* Henry thought to himself as he chuckled, realizing he sounded like an old man cursing the neighborhood kids.

Henry turned around and began to walk away when another knock came from the door.

Henry turned back around and slung the door open.

Nobody.

"What the hell," he thought. He peeked his head out the door and looked over to the left. He caught a glimpse of a man standing at the end of the combined deck of the apartments, his back to Henry, leaning over the railing. This didn't look like Henry's neighbor, Thomas. "Hey! You! Did you knock on my door?" Henry called out to the man.

The man turned around and stared at Henry. Even though the sun was out and shining bright, the man's face was clouded with shadows. Henry couldn't make out a single feature of his face.

The man reached his arm out and pointed a long, scraggly finger nail at Henry and beckoned to him to come closer.

"Come here Henry, we need to talk," the man said.

"Oh, hell no," Henry said to the man.

The man, still silent, began walking towards him. Even as he got closer, Henry still couldn't make out any features of the man, except for odd clothes. He was dressed in all black. Henry turned around and went back into his apartment, slamming the door shut behind him and locking all the locks. *"Who the fuck is that?"* he wondered to himself. Thomas and Bella, his neighbors, were out of town and they weren't supposed to be home until the end of the week. Henry hoped this person wasn't a burglar.

Henry heard three powerful raps at the door, the first causing him to jump away. He looked through the peephole to see the man's shadowed face staring back at him. Henry took a few steps back as the man began to shake the door handle. Henry ran into his room, searching for his pistol to try and defend himself if the man got in. He could still hear the door knob jiggling. As he loaded his .38 Special, slowly sliding five brass bullets into the cylinder, he took off and slid under the island in his kitchen.

The jiggling stopped. Henry stayed put for a few minutes. He was breathing slowly and quietly, his pistol coldly in his hand, and his finger readied around the trigger guard. Then five loud knocks come from the door again. "GO AWAY!" Henry shouted as he came out from underneath the counter, ready to shoot.

"Henry! It's me!" Leonard called out from the other side of the door.

"Leo?" Henry replied as he approached the door. Looking through the peephole he could see his brother's tall and lanky body, spotty goatee, and puffy brown hair. "Man, you scared me," Henry said through the door as he unlocked the door and opened it for his brother.

"Scared you? What, did you think I was the boogeyman," Leonard joked as he held his hands up in the shape of claws and turned his body into a monster pose.

"No, you kept banging on the door and jiggling the door handle like you were trying to break in."

"Nah man, I just knocked on the door a few times," Leonard said, puzzled at his brother's seemingly irrational fear. He looked into his brother's eyes and saw his black pupils almost the size of the brown iris of his eye. Leonard's eyes made their way down to the pistol his brother clinched in his hand.

"What the hell is that for?" He asked, pointing down at the gun and taking a step back towards the door.

"I told you," Henry started, thinking about the featureless figure who stood on his deck minutes ago. "I thought someone was trying to break in."

"There was a guy outside asking for money," Henry continued. "So, I gave it to him. He came back a few minutes later and kept ding dong-ditching me," Henry stopped for a minute, wondering how his brother hadn't seen the man on his way to Henry's apartment. "I walked out and he tried getting in the house," Henry said, half telling the truth and half lying. His mind went back to the featureless man, clothed in all black. He was dressed to the nines, in a black suit, with a black shirt, black dress shoes, and a black bow tie.

"Anyways," Henry spoke up, laying the pistol down on the kitchen table to ease his brother's worries. "Whatcha doing Leo? I thought you were going to Tracy's?"

"I am, but we need to talk," Leonard said as his face and tone quickly turned stern.

"About what?" Henry asked nervously.

"I've been short a few pills every time you've brought me a refill, Henry. Five, six, three, different amounts each time. I mentioned it to Mom, and she thinks something's off too. I know you dropped some the first time, but what about the other times?"

"What're you talking about? If you've been short, why haven't you said anything? I would have started to count them when I picked them up man."

"Henry, the pharmacy doesn't mess up that many times and that inconsistently. Are you taking my pills?" Leonard asked, looking deep into Henry's eyes painted black by his pupils.

"Really Leo? You think I've been stealing from you? Come on man," Henry said, still somehow frustrated by his brother's accusations. He turned around and began walking back to the couch and sat back down, slipping his shoes off and throwing his legs up across the couch. "I'm not a druggy Leo," Henry finished.

"You know there was that rumor after you left high school that you sold drugs."

"Oh, you know that was a bullshit rumor Leo. You and I joke about it all the time."

"Yeah I thought so. Not so sure now."

Henry felt the pills kicking in hard now, as his vision became blurry, his breaths became shallow, and the room began to spin in a flashing light. "Come on Leo, this is bullshit. I can't believe you're even accusing me of this," Henry slurred.

"Don't fucking lie to me Henry," Leonard snapped. "Your pupils are huge, you thought someone was banging at your door, you're sweating like a whore in church, and you're slurring your words."

"I've had a few drinks since I got home. Maybe I'm a little tipsier than I thought," Henry lied.

Leonard made his way to the kitchen to grab a drink. As he leaned into the fridge to grab a soda, he glanced at the trash can. Empty. Henry hadn't drunk anything- there were no beer bottles or cans in the trash can or around the clean and orderly house; there was no glass in the shining sink or in the spic and span living room for a mixed drink. "Henry, stop lying to me."

Henry was starting to become irritated with Leonard now. *"Just mind your own damn business,"* Henry thought to himself.

"Did you seriously just come over here to give me the third-degree Leo?" Henry snapped at Leonard, feeling himself getting angry. He wasn't sure if it was the pills or his bipolar making him mad at Leonard, even though he was right.

"Henry, I'm worried about you man. I know you've been going through a lot, I just don't want you to turn to pills to solve your problems."

"That's fucking ridiculous Leo. Accusing your own brother of stealing pills from you. Really?"

"Henry, stop the charade and tell me the truth."

"You want the truth, Leo?" Henry asked as he reached down to grab one of his shoes. "How's this for the fucking truth?" Henry reared back and hurled his shoe at Leonard.

Leonard, still in his sling and a little less mobile than normal, managed to duck out of the way of the shoe flying towards him like a bullet.

SMASH!

The shoe flew over Leonard's head and smashed through the kitchen window, sending glass flying onto the outside deck.

"What the fuck Henry!" Leonard called out to his brother laying on the couch.

"Just get the hell out Leo," Henry slurred, now feeling the pills more fiercely. He was confused now, almost forgetting that he had just shattered the window in his kitchen.

"I'm not going anywhere Henry. I refuse to leave you like this," Leonard said, staring at his brother nodding off on the couch. "Look at you Henry! You're about to fall asleep in the middle of an argument, after you just shattered a window. You can't honestly expect me to believe you aren't high right now."

"Shattered a window?" Henry said as his head bobbed up and down like a fishing lure in the water. "You're crazy Leo."

Leonard walked to the shattered window and picked up a handful of glass shards from the ground. He walked over to where his brother was struggling to stay awake. "Shattered. Glass." Leonard said intensely, waving his hand in front of his brother's ghost-like face.

Henry looked at his brother's hands cupped together. The glass shards in his hands shimmered in the flashing light around him like he had scooped water out of the sink. Henry saw his face staring back at him- paper white, his eyes sunk back into his head, pupils so large that they looked like holes in his eyes. His face had become nearly featureless.

"Did... did I do that? For real?" Henry stammered, looking up at his brother. His vision was blurred, and he couldn't see Leo's expression. Was he mad? Was he upset? Was he indifferent? Henry couldn't tell.

"Henry, tell me the truth. Have you been stealing my pills?" Leonard calmly asked, staring deep into the blackness swallowing Henry alive.

Henry knew that admitting he had been stealing from his brother would cause a rift between them, and possibly cause him to lose his brother's trust. *"What if Leo tells Mom?"* he thought to himself. *"Would they try to send me to rehab?"*

Despite the compelling reasons NOT to tell the truth, he knew he had to be upfront with his brother now. "Yes," Henry quietly said, as he shifted his eyes from the shattered glass to the one shoe on the ground.

"I thought they would make me feel better. I've been really bad off lately, because of the stress of the new job and managing my money," he said with long, drawn out words. "I couldn't figure out how to get rid of the pain. It has just been a constant pit within me that feels like a black hole. I feel like I'm going to implode. The pills, they made the pain go away."

"They made the pain go away? Temporarily. It's a temporary high, Henry. You should have come to me."

"I didn't want to bother you Leo. You've got a lot going on right now after the surgery. I'm so pissed at dad for what happened to you, he ruined your career."

"Henry, everything happens for a reason man. Maybe I'm not meant to play baseball, only God knows what I'm meant to do. I love you man, you're not just my big brother. You're my best friend," Leonard said as he laid the glass down on the coffee table and bent down to be eye level with Henry. "You're my best friend and I don't want you to struggle alone. You'll never be a burden on me, man."

"You're my little brother and I just want to protect you," Henry stammered, trying to hold his tears back. "I don't want to hurt you either man. You're my best friend too, you're going to be the best man at my wedding- if I ever get married," he chuckled.

"Promise me you won't do this again."

"I promise Leo. I'm sorry," Henry said looking down at his shaking hands.

"Remember Henry," Leonard said as he rolled up his right sleeve to reveal his tattoo on his inner bicep. "Brothers never let each other wander in the dark alone. No matter what you're going through, no matter what I'm going through, our darkest of times, we will be there to lead each other out of the darkness into the light. I love you, man."

Leonard leaned over and wrapped his arms around his older brother. After years of Henry protecting him from the neighborhood bullies who made fun of him for his glasses, helping him through high school heartbreaks, and tutoring him in school, it was his turn to protect his older brother. Leonard knew his brother struggled with depression and bipolar, but he would always be Leonard's big brother and best friend and that would never change. He hated seeing his brother in a dark place.

Henry felt his brother's arms wrap around him. They weren't typically affectionate towards each other. It filled Henry with a sense of honesty and comfort.

His little brother was truly his best friend. Although they had fought a lot when they were younger, he couldn't ask for a better friend now that they were older. All he wanted was to see his brother successful and happy. Seeing his brother so worried about him, though, made him realize that his brother would be happy when Henry was happy. He knew that if his brother had turned to pills, he would do anything and everything he could to help him. He had seen his brother in some dark places, and now his brother saw him in a dark place.

The two boys sat there as they heard the rain start outside. While the rain pounded the roof of Henry's apartment, the two drowned out the sound of the rain with their own thoughts.

The bond between two brothers is unbreakable. They protect each other and look over each other. Through thick and thin, brothers were always there for one another.

They were brothers. They were best friends. They were each other's hero. Nobody could take that from them.

"Be safe going to Tracy's," Henry said as he leaned back against the couch.

"Be safe during these battles, Henry," Leonard responded, looking at his brother with care and love.

PART 4:
THOMAS CLARK &
BELLA MORGAN
TWO YEARS AGO

- - - - -

Henry pulled into the parking lot of his apartment complex, only to find that someone had parked in his designated spot. This was becoming a regular occurrence; his downstairs neighbor had been taking his spot after long nights of drinking. Henry was getting frustrated with this. It was the principle of the matter and not that it really inconvenienced him.

As Henry made his way to the visitor parking lot to park his car, he had an idea. After he parked his car, he hurriedly made his way to his apartment. He ran up the stairs of his apartment and knocked on the door to the apartment beside his.

"Why do you have a shit-eating grin on your face?" Bella Morgan, one of Henry's best friends and girlfriend to Henry's longtime friend Thomas Clark, said in her usual sarcastic tone.

Bella was an average height girl, with olive skin, and short dark black hair that she dyed once a month to stay 'current'. Her body was littered with tattoos, and the two were in a competition to see who could get more. Bella always sounded like she was pissed off, but Henry had learned to just deal with it. Even though she could be aggravating, she had become Henry's safe person and he always went to her when he struggled with his mental health.

"So, you know how 128 has been taking my parking spot lately?" Henry beamed. They didn't know the name of Henry's downstairs neighbor, so they just called him by his apartment number.

"You're still going on about this shit Henry?" She asked, dismissively.

"Yes! It's the principle of the matter Bella. He thinks he can just park there because he's drunk. I have a solution!"

"Oh God," Bella snorted. "THOMAS!" She bellowed.

Thomas came around the corner from the bathroom- Henry assuming he had just taken his hourly shit- to meet the two at the door.

Thomas was about Henry's height, more on the heavyset side, and strong as an ox. He was as country as country comes, a stereotypical redneck. He had a bushy brown beard down to his chest and proudly wore a mullet.

He drove a jacked-up Chevy truck with big tires and rims, spoke in a country accent, owned more guns than the entire Confederate Army, and loved fishing and hunting. Henry and Thomas had become pretty much brothers by now. Henry had been there for Thomas when his mother passed away, and Thomas had been the one to convince Henry to go see a doctor about his mood swings.

After they graduated from college, Henry and Lisa had gone their separate ways. They still talked occasionally but weren't nearly as close as they once were. Lisa left Henry behind and took a job in Tennessee and Henry took a part-time financial planner job in his hometown. Since taking the part-time job, he had swiftly progressed into a higher-level financial position. Henry missed her friendship but was lucky that he met Thomas when he did.

"Hey Henry," He said, yawning.

"Hey Thom. I think you'll appreciate this buddy. So tonight, while 128 is out partying, I'm going to sneak down the road to the construction zone." Bella and Thomas looked at each other, knowing this was another one of Henry's half-baked schemes. "I'm going to take a traffic cone, put it in the spot, and put a sign on it that says, 'Parking For I25 ONLY.'"

"You're an idiot," Bella lashed at Henry.

"I love it!" Thomas shouted, high fiving Henry in the process. Thomas and Henry were partners in crime, always doing stupid stuff together around town and always having a blast doing it.

"Oh, I knew you would!" Henry said, slapping his friend on the back.

"Of course you would. You're both idiots," Bella said as she rolled her eyes.

- - - - -

As night rolled around, Henry heard 128's car crank up and pull out of the parking lot. *"This is my chance,"* Henry thought to himself. Henry finished his fifth beer of the night, dulling his nerves and giving him liquid courage to go forth with his plan.

He was wearing all black- a black Carhartt jacket big enough to hide the cone in, black jeans, black shoes, and a black beanie. He walked out his door and checked the parking space to make sure 128 had left. It was a warm Carolina night out, still 78 degrees at 10 o'clock. Henry was already sweating.

He took off down the steps and made his way to the main road. *"He's either going to respect the cone or just move it. Either way, I'm sure he will get the point,"* Henry thought as he made his way down the sidewalk towards a nearby road construction area.

As Henry approached the construction zone, he spotted a traffic cone situated far enough away from the rest that it wouldn't cause any inconveniences to the construction crew or cause any drivers to damage their cars. Even with his half-baked scheme, he was still trying to be courteous of those who hadn't wronged him, unlike 128. He snuck over to the cone and picked it up, slipping it in between his sweat covered body and coat.

As Henry looked up to make sure nobody saw him, he caught the glimpse of a man in the distance looking right at him underneath a tall street light. The man was short and stubby, almost the same height and size of Henry. He squinted to try and get a better look at the man but couldn't make him out. Henry decided the man was far enough away for him to take off and not be caught.

As Henry took off down the sidewalk towards his apartment complex, lugging the cone underneath his jacket, a voice called out to him like the wind in the middle of the night, **"Henry, come back."**

He looked over his shoulder to see if the man was following him. Henry came to a halt and turned around, realizing that the man who was watching him had disappeared into the night. Henry began to look around the construction zone and the sidewalk to see if he could spot the man or whoever had spoken his name, but to no avail.

"Weird," Henry thought to himself.

Henry made his way back to his apartment complex, stopping in front of his designated parking spot. Henry knew he could easily just pull his Mustang back into his spot, but decided that wouldn't get his point across.

He slid the cone from underneath his coat and placed it centered in the spot. He pulled out the laminated sheet he made earlier in the day and slipped it in the slit on top of the cone. He looked over his handiwork, beaming with pride.

"That'll do it donkey!" Henry thought to himself, using one of his newfound catch phrases that nobody really understood except him.

153

As Henry was preparing to go back inside, he heard yelling and the sound of crashing dishes coming from Bella and Thomas' apartment. Worried, he frantically made his way up the steps to their door. As he approached the door and reached out to knock, it flung open revealing Bella with her mascara smeared down her cheeks and an angry look painting the area around her face not smeared with makeup. She held a tote bag between her arms like a giant teddy bear.

"Hey Henry," she said, trying to give off the impression that nothing was wrong.

"What's wrong Bella? What's going on? Are you okay?" Henry asked.

"I just can't do it anymore. He doesn't love me like I thought. He doesn't take it seriously. He's just an asshole."

"What? Thom loves you Bell," Henry said in a concerned tone.

"Let her go Henry," Thomas shouted, slurring his words, from inside the apartment. "If she doesn't think I love her, she can go."

"THOMAS! I used to fucking believe you loved me, but not anymore, you asshole! You're just not serious about it. I want to be with someone who wants to marry me, wants to have children with me, someone who values me!" Bella screamed back with tears welling up in her eyes as she pushed past Henry.

"Bell, wait," Henry called out, reaching for his friend.

"Henry, I can't right now. I'll text you tomorrow and we can talk about it. I just can't be around that asshole right now," she said through sobs.

Henry watched as Bella made her way down the flight of stairs, looking back and forth between her and Thomas standing in his apartment. "Thom, what is going on?" Henry asked as he walked into the apartment and closed the door behind him.

"I don't know man," Thomas slurred as he turned, nearly losing his balance, to look at Henry entering the threshold. "She just started talking about me not being serious about our relationship and not wanting to get married or have kids or blah, blah, blah. Same shit she just said. It's dumb and I'm done fighting with her about it."

"We've talked about y'all getting married a ton, why does she think that?"

"Because I don't 'express myself' enough," Thomas said in a frustrated and sarcastic tone.

"Just let her blow it off tonight and try talking to her tomorrow man," Henry said, putting his hand on his friend's shoulder in an attempt to calm him down.

"I think this is it," Thomas said, slumping into his couch and closing his eyes.

- - - - -

[Bell, Thom does love you.] Henry texted.

[Not like I thought Henry.] Bella replied.

[Bella, please come back. It isn't the same without you at the apartment complex, it's eerie. I miss you and so does Thom.]

[Henry.] [I cant.]

[Bell, please. I need you, you're my safe person.]

[And I always will be Henry despite what happens between me and Thomas. You and I were the best of friends.]

[But Bella, you and Thom are meant to be. I promise he loves you, and I know you love him.] Henry texted. She didn't reply.

- - - - -

157

Henry woke up to the sound of clanging and banging coming from his neighbor's apartment. Bella and Thomas had been split up for nearly a week now, but most of her stuff was still in the apartment. Henry took that as a sure-fire sign they would get back together.

As Henry got up and walked outside, he saw a U-Haul in the parking lot and Bella carrying boxes out of the apartment.

"Where you going Bell?" Henry said as he yawned and stretched.

"I'm just getting all my shit out of the apartment Henry," she coldly replied.

"Yeah, she's going back to Kenny's house," Thomas shouted from inside the apartment. Kenny was Bella's ex, one that had been abusive both physically and mentally towards Bella in the past. He and Henry had bad blood in the past, before Henry had ever met Bella. Henry instinctively snarled at the sound of his name.

"Dammit Thomas, I told you Kenny is actually serious about our relationship!" Bella yelled back, clearly irritated.

"Bell, the guy is a fraud. He's putting on a facade to make you think he cares, like he has always done," Henry quietly said to her.

"No, I think he's really different this time Henry," Bella said. She refused to make eye contact with Henry. She clearly didn't believe what she was saying either.

"Bell come on," Henry pleaded as he reached out to hug her.

Bella rested her head on Henry's shoulder, sobbing, and said "Henry, I love Thomas. I just don't feel like he's serious right now. I'm not sure I'm IN love with him right now. Maybe one day, but just not now."

As Henry rubbed his friend's back, knowing there was no changing her mind at this point, he whispered to her "Just be careful Bell."

"I will Henry," she promised him.

"Here," Thomas said as he crossed the threshold of his apartment into the daylight. "You asked me to write you a letter a few months ago telling you how I felt. Well I wrote it. I was looking for the best time to give it to you. Guess now is as good a time as any." Thomas pulled out a folded, crumpled piece of notebook paper, with the frills still hanging off the edges, and handed it to Bella before turning around and going back into his apartment and slamming the door shut.

Bella, shutting her eyes to hold the tears in, let go of Henry and took her last box and the crumpled piece of paper back to the truck. As she got in the truck, she turned and looked up at Henry looking down at her, with a single glistening tear appearing from her eye. "I'm still your safe person Henry," she called out.

- - - - -

Bella laid her head against the window of the U-Haul truck as Kenny put it in drive and left the apartment complex in the distance. She wanted to read the letter but knew it would set Kenny off if she read it in front of him.

"'Swrong with you Bella," Kenny asked her coldly.

"I'm just tired, I tried staying up waiting for you last night," Bella said, not sure if she was trying to convince Kenny or herself of the lie she had just told.

"I'm sorry, the soccer game ran late. The tournament ends tonight. You're coming, right?"

"Yeah, I planned on it," she said, this time compensating for the lie she had told.

"Good," Kenny said, reaching over and roughly grabbing Bella's hand. Bella looked down at her hand and felt Kenny's tightening grip around it.

"All Kenny cares about is getting drunk, playing soccer with his useless friends, and controlling someone," she thought to herself. She subtly shook her head, trying to get that thought out of her head. *"No, this is the right decision. He's serious this time. He told me he wanted to marry me."*

Bella came off as irritable and rude, but really all she wanted was a family. Growing up, her father would beat her if she didn't come home with at least a B in school, or when she had a bad volleyball game. She knew that as soon as she walked into the door, she would hear the whirring of her dad pulling his belt swiftly from around his waist. Her mom left her when she was a five, to go live with her secret lover. She would never forget her mom, with a suitcase tucked under her home, leaning down to her and saying, "As long as you're the sperm of your dad, you'll be useless."

She lacked the loving family she yearned so badly for. She thought she had found her family with Thomas and Henry, but lately Thomas had been so distant. It was like he didn't care anymore.

She and Henry had been arguing a lot lately too. She knew Henry was struggling to keep his bipolar under control, but she couldn't help but to be combative at times. She knew Henry didn't mean any harm, and she hoped he knew that she didn't either. He was truly her best friend- her brother, really.

- - - - -

Thomas sat down on his couch and cracked open another beer, turning on the TV to the day's football game. *"I can't believe she went back to Kenny, of all people,"* he thought to himself. He had found out she was back with Kenny by accident when he saw a Snapchat of her at his house.

Thomas heard a knock at his door and yelled out
"Come in, it's unlocked!" as he ran his hand down to the
pistol he always kept snugged in between his waistband to be
prepared for an intruder.

"You alright Thom?" Henry called out as he walked
through the door.

"Yeah, I'm fine," Thomas lied as he took his hand off
the pistol.

"You don't look fine," Henry said, looking around the
living room that looked more like a landfill covered in beer
bottles and cans. Henry's mind couldn't stand the mess, so
he found a trash bag underneath Thomas's sink and began
picking up the cans and bottles.

"I'm good. Her loss," Thomas said, throwing his
hands up in the air, spilling a splash of beer on the couch in
the process. He looked over at Henry cleaning up his mess
and chuckled to himself *"That's Henry's way of dealing with
stress."*

"She'll be back man, Kenny is going to pull his same old shit and she will be back," Henry said as he picked up his fifteenth bottle and seventh can, admiring the ocean of bottles and cans still left around the apartment.

"It's whatever," Thomas said, turning his attention back to the TV. He couldn't focus on the TV; his mind kept wandering back to the way Bella looked when she was leaving. Thomas had a way of reading people's eyes and he swore that she still loved him. *"Why did she leave then?"*

Thomas wasn't good with communicating his feelings, it just wasn't who he was. He glanced over at Henry, now filling up his third trash bag, and chuckled to himself again. He leaned on Henry to be his voice of reason a lot; he always seemed to have the right answers. He had taken Henry with him to look at engagement rings for Bella. Henry kept telling him to tell her how he really felt about her, and he hadn't listened. Henry was the best friend - no, brother - a guy could ask for.

- - - - -

As Bella sat on the cold, hard bleachers in the forty-degree weather- Carolina weather was weird, freezing one day and hot as hades the next-, she looked down at her phone to see Henry calling her. *"Not now Henry,"* she thought to herself as she ignored his call.

Bella turned around to breathe into her hands to warm them up. As she turned to face the wood line next to the soccer field, she saw a shadow moving gracefully through the brush. Bella squinted as she tried to make it out.

"Trish, you mind running to the store to grab me and the guys some more beer?" Bella heard Kenny call out to one of the girls watching the soccer game, causing her to switch her attention back to the field.

"Sure KennyPoo!" Trisha shouted back, with a dumb smile painted across her caked, bimbo face.

"Bleh. KennyPoo? Really? And Kenny, are you even going to ask me if I want anything?" Bella thought to herself as she scowled at Trisha and waited for Kenny to at least acknowledge her presence.

"Thanks, you're a doll Trish," Kenny said as he winked at her and backpedaled onto the field to resume his soccer and beer drinking.

Bella looked down at her phone as it rang again. *"Henry, not now!"* she thought as she rejected his call again.

Remembering that she had seen something in the woods, she turned her attention again towards the tree line. She caught a glimmer of blue sparkling from the woods. What could it be? A lost puppy? A rabbit? A deer? *"Bigfoot?"* she thought and giggled. Bella loved animals, and the idea of Bigfoot.

As Bella reached into her pocket to pull out her cigarettes, the note that Thomas had given her earlier that day fell out onto the cold bleachers. Bella stared at the crumpled, folded piece of paper wondering what she should do with it. She looked back up at Kenny, watching him laugh and joke with the rest of the guys on his soccer team and various girls and wives of the other players. Not once since they had gotten there had Kenny even remotely acknowledged her presence. Bella didn't even know why she came. She hated soccer.

She looked back down at her phone to see three texts from Henry reading *[Plz call]*, *[Bell plz]*, *[Need talk]*. Henry was normally proper with his texts, not using slang like this. *"Henry, I'll call you in a minute,"* she thought to herself almost in an attempt to communicate telepathically.

Bella unfolded the piece of paper and began to read the scrappy handwritten note scribbled on it.

"Bella,

You know I'm not good with words, so please bear with me on this. You asked me last night to write you a letter telling you what you mean to me. I've been sitting in my truck all day, trying to figure out what to say and how to say it.

Honestly, I'm still at a loss, but I'm going to give it my all here. When I look into your eyes, I see me and you rocking in rocking chairs on a porch. We're grey-haired, cranky, and old. However, our love is stronger than ever.

I look at the rounds of your cheeks and the dimples in your smile and I think of our children laughing and playing. I see them riding on my back while I pretend to be a horse. I see you nurturing and caring for them like the best mother I have ever seen. Again, our love is growing every day.

When I see the way your face lights up any room you enter, I see you walking down the aisle in a beautiful

169

white dress. You're carrying a bouquet of flowers and all eyes are on you, step by step you make your way towards me. My eyes begin to blur with tears because you're so radiant. Our love for one another still grows.

Bella, what you mean to me is my life. You mean happiness and a life worth living. You mean smiles and kisses full of love and laughter. You mean the next 'Mrs. Clark' walking down the aisle. You mean little Bella and Thomas' running around a crowded living room. You mean hand in hand, rocking in a rocking chair as the sun sets on our lives. You mean love.

Yours truly,
Papa Bear"

With tears in her eyes, Bella looked down at her ringing phone. It was Henry, again. "Henry are you okay?" she asked as she answered the phone.

Only deep gasps for air came from the other side of the phone. "Henry! What's wrong?" Bella exclaimed as she jumped off the bleachers and made her way to the parking lot to try and hear Henry better, getting away from the noise of the soccer field.

"Bella?" Henry asked from the other side of the phone.

"Yes, Henry. You called me, are you okay?"

"I… I don't know where I am," Henry said, in a confused and worried tone.

"What do you mean you don't know where you are? What happened?"

"I was driving back home… and now I'm here."

"Henry, where is 'here'? Look around you and tell me what's around you."

Again, only deep gasps for air came from the other side of the phone. Henry sounded like he had been punched in the gut and was struggling to get air. "Lights. Cars." he finally said.

"Henry are you driving? Are you parked? Are you on the road?"

"I… I think I'm parked. In a parking lot maybe? I can't really move. My body feels like cement. My head is so heavy."

"Did you get in an accident?" Bella asked, worriedly. Deep gasps for breath came from the other end of the phone again, as Henry struggled to get air. "Henry, listen to me buddy. I need you to take a deep breath of air, slow your breathing, and listen to my voice."

The other end of the line was silent except for the faint sound of Henry slowly breathing. She was going to let

Henry take a minute to try and calm down, but she had to get to the bottom of what was happening.

Looking up from the asphalt covered with cigarette butts and straw wrappers, she saw the same blue sparkle that she had seen earlier. This time, Bella could make out the outline of a deer staring back at her. She had never seen a deer with such blue eyes, but his gaze captivated her. Both creature's eyes locked with one another. Bella, trying to figure out why the deer's gaze felt so familiar, began to think about Thomas.

Thomas used to look deep into Bella's eyes and say he was reading her soul. She always felt captivated when he did that, he had a way of knowing exactly what her mood was and exactly what she was thinking when he would do that. It seemed strange to imagine, but she felt like the deer was looking into her eyes like Thomas used to when he was reading her soul.

"Bell?" Henry asked again, breaking Bella's focus on the deer.

"Yeah buddy, I'm still here."

"Where are you?" Henry asked quietly.

"I'm at the soccer field," she said, puzzled with his question.

"Is Thom with you? Will you tell Thom I need him to come get me?"

"Henry," Bella started, even more confused now. "Thomas and I aren't together."

"Oh, where is he then?"

"No Henry, I mean Thomas and I aren't dating anymore. We broke up last week, remember?" Why was Henry asking about this? Didn't he know they had broken up?

"Did you guys break up because of me? Did I do something wrong?"

"No Henry, it wasn't you. You don't remember me and Thomas breaking up?"

"No," Henry said quietly. Bella could hear Henry's Mustang coming to life in the background. "I have to go home."

"Henry, stay on the phone with me until you get to the apartment complex, please," Bella pleaded to him.

The phone call ended abruptly.

- - - - -

Thomas looked down at his phone as Bella's name and picture came across the screen. *"Why is she calling me?"*

Thomas scowled to himself. "Hello?" he said, answering the phone in an irritated tone.

"Thomas, is Henry home yet?" She called from the other side of the phone, sounding worried more than anything.

"Uh, I don't know," Thomas said as he got up and walked to the window overlooking the parking lot. Thomas scanned the lot and his eyes connected with Henry's Mustang idling in his parking spot, the traffic cone he stole between his front bumper and the curb. "Yeah, what the hell is going on?" Thomas said as he hurried out the door.

"Thomas be easy. I think he had a really bad panic attack. He called me a bunch and texted me, and when I talked to him, he didn't know where he was," Bella stopped before telling him the rest of what happened. "He didn't remember we were broken up Thomas," she finally had the courage to say.

"What do you mean? He was here when we broke up, he was here earlier today when you were getting all of your stuff?" Thomas said as he made his way down the steps of the apartment complex.

"Sometimes, in periods of high stress, panic attacks can make a person go back to their last happy memory. Henry was upset about us breaking up, he probably stressed himself out about it. You know he worries about us more than he does himself," Bella whispered into the phone.

"He was in the apartment earlier cleaning up my mess. You know that's how he deals with stress. Only reason he left was because he had dinner plans with some coworkers..." Thomas began before abruptly stopping his sentence.

"Oh God Bell," Thomas stammered. "Henry's car is running, but he's not in it."

- - - - -

"He... Help. Help me," Henry gasped out. He was laying on his back porch, drenched in a spilt beer. The beer must have been full, because there was so much puddled around him and seeping into his shirt and pants.

How had he gotten here? Why was he laying on the ground? Why was he cold and sticky? Henry struggled to figure out what had led him to where he was as his entire body began to shiver uncontrollably. Henry's mind was slipping away, and he began to claw at his face and ears, trying to pull the thoughts and the pain out of his own mind.

Suddenly, Henry was looking at his own pitiful body lying on his back porch. Henry felt like an omniscient spirit, overlooking his own soaked body. He was watching the poor soul below him scraping his face and ears with dull fingernails. Henry tried to call out to himself and put him at ease, but it did no good.

Then, Henry saw the glass door to his porch slide open. Was it Thomas or Bella coming to his rescue? He watched a man swallowed in the darkness of the night sky walk onto the back porch. The man was short and stout, eerily similar to the man Henry had seen last week at the construction zone.

The man stood over Henry's body and looked down on him, cocking his head to one side or the other as he attempted to see what was wrong. The man reached a hand out towards Henry's body, still scratching and clawing at himself.

Henry closed his eyes so that he wouldn't have to see his own body in such a miserable position.

- - - - -

Henry opened his eyes and was overlooking his porch once again, now leaned up against the railing. He had returned to his body, but now he couldn't feel anything. No emotion, no pain, no feeling at all. He was but a shell. His whole body was cold. This was what he imagined death felt like. At that moment, Henry was just a lifeless body struggling for air.

"Henry!" he could hear Thomas call out. "Henry, where are you?"

Henry made every effort he could to yell out 'I'm here!', but he could only get out small gasps of air and silent words in between. He could hear a banging on the door of his apartment, and all he wanted to do was yell out 'Come in, the doors unlocked.' The knocking at his door got quieter and quieter as the numbness crept back into Henry's body.

He could slowly see and breathe again, his heart rate had slowed down to a normal speed, the tears were wiped away from his eyes, and everything was fine. On the outside. Henry's mind kept accelerating.

His mind seemed like an old VHS tape. He kept fast forwarding the VHS tape to get back to where his life had left off, but he had to go through all of the parts he had already seen. While the VHS fast forwarded, it would occasional get stuck, stopping at triggering moments that caused the black hole in his chest to increase and his mind to wonder those dreadful 'What If?' questions. 'What if I hadn't done that?' or 'What if I hadn't said that to that person?'

As his mind began to get back to the present, he began to relive what had happened up to this point. He saw himself begin to have a panic attack while he was driving, calling Bella in the parking lot of the grocery store, pulling into his apartment and running over something, making his way into his apartment, opening a beer to calm him down, falling over as his panic increased, and overlooking his pitiful body as someone moved him.

The movie came to an end and the TV turned off, as Henry blacked out and rested his head against the railing of his porch.

- - - - -

"Oh God Henry, where are you? Please be okay," Bella thought to herself as she drove to her former apartment complex. *"Henry, please be okay. Please don't hurt yourself. I need you. We need you. So many people need you, you sweet soul. Please Henry."*

As Bella pulled into the apartment complex, she could see Thomas frantically beating on the door to Henry's apartment. She pulled up behind Henry's idling car, the traffic cone stuck in between it and the curve, and hurriedly got out and ran up the steps. "Is he in there?" She called out to Thomas as she approached the door.

"I don't know," he said as he turned back around to pound on the door again. "I've searched all over the complex and can't find him. He has to be in there."

"God Henry, what are you doing," Bella thought aloud as she tried to look through the blinds of Henry's window. "Have you tried the door yet? Are you sure it's locked?" Bella asked, looking over at Thomas.

Thomas, realizing that he had missed the simplest thing, looked down at the door knob. Henry rarely locked his door if he was home. He reached out and turned the door knob and felt it unlatch itself from the door frame. "Oops," Thomas said nervously as he looked at Bella.

"You fucking buffoon," she cracked as she made her way past Thomas, stopping to turn and look deep into Thomas' eyes, and into Henry's apartment. "You better hope he's okay and we aren't too late you idiot!"

"Do you see him?" Thomas asked as he crossed the threshold, clearly ignoring Bella's frustrations. He spotted Bella coming out of Henry's room and looking in his direction.

"No," she said quietly, pale as a ghost, struck with fear.

Thomas looked deep into Bella's eyes, seeing her soul appearing from within. He could tell she was worried about Henry. So was he. But he also saw that she had read his letter.

Henry had struggled with some massive panic attacks before, but never one this bad. He had never seen Henry forget a week's worth of memories during an episode, nor disappear like this. He knew he had to find him before something terrible happened.

Thomas glanced past Bella's shoulder and looked at the glass door leading to Henry's back porch. It was cracked open slightly. "There!" Thomas shouted as he pointed at the back porch and pushed past Bella.

Bella whirled around to see where Thomas was going. She saw Thomas sliding the glass door open and running to the corner of the back porch. She could make out the figure of Henry's body, slumped against the railings of the deck, soaking wet, seemingly lifeless as Thomas lifted him up and brought him out of the cold. "Henry," Bella whimpered to herself.

- - - - -

Henry slowly opened his eyes, staring at his ceiling. His body still felt numb and lifeless, but he could hear the whirling sound of the fan overhead and could finally feel the air expanding in his lungs. He heard the sound of a toilet flush and slowly turned his head. He instantly knew Thomas must be there, taking his hourly shit.

"Hey buddy," Thomas said, making his way out of the bathroom, seeing Henry's eyes slowly open. Henry didn't say anything back and just blinked a few times to acknowledge that he had heard Thomas.

"Is he awake?" He heard Bella's voice call from the kitchen, as she approached where he was laying. "You okay buddy?" she asked as she sat down on the edge of the couch with Henry.

Henry, again without saying anything, slowly nodded his head in acknowledgment of Bella's question.

"Henry, what happened?" Thomas asked, in a more serious tone.

"I don't know," he finally said. It was the first he had spoken since coming to, and the first words he felt like he had said in years. "I left the steakhouse and was headed home. I felt a panic attack coming on, my heart started beating fast, I started sweating a lot, I was shaking. I just wanted to make it home. From there, though, it's just blurs. I remember calling and texting you Bell," Henry closed his eyes as he paused, trying to remember more of what had transpired. "I remember asking you if Thom was with you and being confused when you told me y'all broke up. For some reason, I had forgotten that. I'm sorry. I'm sorry I forgot that. I remember pulling up into my parking spot and thinking I had hit someone because I ran over the cone. Then I remember lying face down on the back porch and

Thomas coming out there and picking me up to put me against the railings,"

"Henry," Thomas interrupted, leaning against the door frame of the living room. "I didn't pick you up and put you against the railing."

"Somebody picked me up, I saw it. I felt it."

"Nobody came in. I was standing out at your door ever since I noticed you were home. When I found you, you were leaning up against the railing, not face down."

"No, I'm telling you. Some guy, about my size, came in and picked me up off the ground and leaned me against the railing. I honestly thought it was you Thomas. It helped me breathe," Henry said, convinced that someone had come in to help him.

"Okay buddy," Thomas said, realizing that it wasn't worth trying to convince him otherwise.

Thomas made his way over to where Henry and Bella were and put his arm around Bella's shoulder. Thomas, seeing the confused look on Henry's face, said "We talked it over," as he looked down at Bella. "We both need to do better communicating with one another."

"After I read his letter, I realized he was serious about us, and maybe he wasn't such an asshole. After seeing the way he cared about you and was worried about you the same way I was, I realized I couldn't leave you two buffoons behind. I miss you guys too much," Bella said as she felt the tears coming and laid her head in the crevice of Thomas' shoulder and chest. "Henry, we love you. We would be lost without you. Don't you dare scare us like this again, you asshole."

Henry lifted his arm up slowly and balled his fist up. Thomas and Bella looked at each other, confused. Henry turned his balled-up fist around and lifted his middle finger up at the two, cracking a smile while he did. "I love you guys too," he coughed.

"You're an ass," Bella laughed as she playfully slapped Henry's hand out the air.

Henry smiled as he looked at two of his best friends sitting by his side. He could tell they had been worried mere hours before. Bella was still pale as a ghost and Thomas' mullet was in a frizz. His friends- nay, his family- loved him. He loved them too, more than he loved himself at times. His heart hurt when things went south between them, and he was sure that was what led to his panic attack.

During the panic attack, his mind instantly transported him back to the last happy moment he had- standing on the porch with Bella and Thomas, telling them about his plan to get I28. Somehow, Henry's panic attack had brought them together again and helped them see that each one loved the other. His family was back together, and that's all he needed at that moment.

Henry sat up and put his arms around Bella and Thomas, pulling them in closer. "Thank y'all," he started. "For being my family."

PART 5:
ABBY CHILDE
ONE YEAR AGO

- - - - -

Henry rolled over in his bed and opened his eyes to see his fiancé, Abby Childe, still sleeping peacefully beside him. She was a stunning girl, with blazing red hair, a face full of freckles, a smile that would light up the midnight sky, and a voice like an angel. She was so radiant that the first time Henry saw her, he had to check his pulse to make sure he wasn't seeing an angel in Heaven. Henry gazed in her deep, earthy brown eyes as she opened them. Her eyes glistened like skyscrapers in the New York skyline. Her eyes held secrets that would drive an ordinary person insane. Her eyes held Henry's secrets.

"Hello there handsome," she whispered in her angelic voice as she smiled at him. "How did you sleep?"

"Fantastic being next to you," Henry smiled back. Abby had moved in with Henry nearly a month ago now. Waking up next to her and seeing her peacefully sleeping still made every morning worth waking up for. Abby had been away at school two states over throughout their relationship, but having to cherish every second they spent together had only made their love stronger

Abby leaned over and planted a soft kiss onto Henry's cheek, her daily morning gift to him. Henry had proposed to her last year before she left for her senior year of college, and he had never been happier. She came into his life when he finally found the right combination of medicine that made him feel 'good' again, and he took that as a sign from God himself.

Abby got out of bed and found her phone to check the time. "Oh shoot, it's already 8 o'clock!" she yipped as she began to get ready for her morning shift at ten. Since coming back from school, she had taken a job as a waitress at a local chain restaurant while she tried to find a job as a nurse. Henry admired, and appreciated, her dedication to making herself better. She made Henry do the same. He thought the two of them could rule the world if they wanted to.

"What time do you get off tonight, babe?" Henry asked her as he propped himself up on his elbow.

"It depends how busy we are. I'm hoping I can be out of there by 10 o'clock tonight since I'm working a double today," she said, sliding her white t-shirt over the curves of her body. "Do you have any plans for the day?"

"Not that I know of. I might see if Bell and Thom want to go get dinner tonight," Henry responded, already thinking about what sounded good for dinner.

"Okay my love," she sang back in her sweet tone.

Henry looked into her beautiful eyes and smiled as he laid his head back down on his pillow and closed his eyes.

- - - - -

Henry peeked through the blinds of his bedroom window as he watched Abby's car leaving the parking lot of their apartment complex. Abby was his true love and he knew they were meant to be, but often times his anxiety would get the best of him. *"Is she really going to work?"* he would wonder.

"I bet she's going to go cheat on me."

"No, that's just dumb."

"But what if it isn't?"

"Maybe she is going to work, but she has another boyfriend that works there."

"Or a boyfriend that comes to see her at work because he knows I'm not there."

"What if she gets off early every night and goes to her other boyfriend's house?"

His mind would swim with those thoughts until they boiled over. *"STOP! YOU ARE BEING RIDICULOUS!"* he would have to tell himself.

As he let the blinds he was holding open slide against the tips of his fingers and fall shut, his body began to shake. For some reason, his anxiety was especially high today. He couldn't put his finger on it, but he felt a constant feeling of hopelessness creeping throughout his body. It was like a tingling sensation that rang throughout every extremity on his body, like a constant current from a weak live wire. It made his body shiver at first and became more extreme until he felt like he was going into shock.

- - - - -

About noon, Henry heard a knock at his front door. He made his way to the front door. He opened the door to see Bella tapping her foot at the door. "Henry are you going to dinner with us tonight?" she asked, sounding aggravated.

"I was planning on it. What's wrong Bell?" Henry asked back.

"Thomas won't decide where he wants to go eat. He's being a real asshole. We've been going back and forth about where to go for the last hour. 'I don't care, what do you want?' Over and over again. That man can be frustrating sometimes."

"Bella! I can hear you, the window in the kitchen is open!" Thomas jokingly called from within their apartment.

"Guys," Henry laughed. "Let's just go to Uehara's Bistro," Henry said, suggesting their favorite Japanese restaurant in town.

"Ohhh that sounds good," Bella and Thomas said in unison.

"Okay, now that that's solved, what time do y'all want to leave?" Henry asked, instantly regretting his question.

"Let's leave around 6 o'clock," Bella said.

"No, seven!" Thomas called back, sounding closer as he had made his way to the kitchen window so he could better hear the conversation.

"Six-thirty, guys. Six-thirty," Henry laughed again. The three agreed on that time and went their separate ways.

- - - - -

Henry pulled his jeans up to his waist and tried to button them. His hands were shaking, making it more difficult for him to button the already tight jeans. Henry began to get frustrated with himself as his hands shook and the button for his jeans rattled in his hand, struggling to find the slit on the other side to slide into. *"These damn jeans are too tight. I need to lose weight,"* Henry thought to himself, as he blamed his struggles on the jeans and tried to ignore the anxiety overtaking his body.

Henry slipped his current pair of jeans from around his waist and threw them at the wall, frustrated. He walked to his closet to find another pair of jeans to put on. As he pulled out another pair of larger jeans, there was a knock at the door. Henry glanced at the clock sitting on his nightstand and realized it was already six-thirty. "HOLD ON!" he called out.

He realized that he has lost any desire he had to go out with Thomas and Bella. He had a knot in the pit of his stomach at the mere thought out of leaving the apartment. He was going to have to push himself to go now though.

As he struggled to get his hands under control, he slid the new pair of jeans up to his waist and pulled the flaps together. As his hands shook, he managed to slide the button of the jeans into the slit on the other side. *"Finally,"* he thought to himself.

As another knock came from the door, Henry made his way to the door. "HOLD ON I SAID!" he called out.

As he passed the threshold of his bedroom, he bent down to grab his shoes and slide them on. He propped himself up against the door frame and slid his left foot into his left shoe. His shakiness made it hard to keep his balance. As he reached up to slide his right shoe on, Henry lost his balance and went plummeting to the ground, landing with a loud thud.

Henry's front door flung open as Thomas came running in after hearing the sound of Henry falling. Thomas looked down at Henry, on his back, half his body in his room and the other half in the hallway, with one shoe on and the other lying beside him. "Having trouble buddy?" Thomas chuckled at the sight.

"Shut up," Henry said as he attempted to lift himself off the ground.

As Henry reached his hand out to his friend, Thomas asked, "Henry, is your blood sugar okay? Are you hydrated? You're shaking pretty bad buddy."

Henry blinked rapidly a few times before responding, "Yeah, I'm fine. Probably just shocked I knocked myself over." Henry rose to his feet and brushed himself off, attempting to also brush off his shakiness. "Let's go, Bell will be pissed if we keep her waiting," Henry halfheartedly laughed as he headed towards the door.

Henry glanced over his shoulder and noticed how far behind him Thomas was. He looked back down at his hands and noticed they were trembling. *"I hope he doesn't notice how bad they're shaking,"* he thought to himself as they slowly made his way down the steps towards Bella's SUV.

As Henry walked down the steps, he had to rebalance himself every couple of steps. He reached out to grab the railing as he reached the bottom of the steps and glanced over at his hand. He hadn't noticed it before, but his hands were extremely pale, in spite of the blaring sun.

As they crawled into Bella's SUV, she yelled out "It's about time, assface." Thomas reached over and lightly touched Bella's arm and gave her a worried look, silently asking for her to ease up on Henry.

"Guys," Henry said as he opened the door of the SUV that he had just closed, already not wanting to deal with going out. "You know what, I'm not feeling good. Y'all go ahead and go. I'm going to go lay down." Henry, having just got into the vehicle, slowly made his way back out. His breathing was becoming more rapid, and he couldn't imagine going anywhere feeling like this. He had begun to feel dizzy when he walked down the steps and was now regretting his decision to go anywhere.

"Are you sure buddy? We can hang out with you if you need," Bella said, clearly concerned about Henry's sudden decision.

"No, it's fine. I'm just going to lay down and take a nap. Y'all go, have fun," Henry replied back, halfheartedly.

"Buddy, you okay?" Thomas asked. He was worried his friend was going to have a panic attack.

"Yeah, just a little tired," Henry said in a not-so-convincing tone. He turned around and began to walk away before his friends could ask him any more questions.

As Henry made his way into his apartment, he felt his anxiety taking over. It wasn't quite a panic attack, but it didn't feel good either. Taking deep breaths and attempting to push out the anxiety-fueled thoughts, he stumbled into his bedroom and made his way to his bed. Technically, he wasn't lying to Thomas and Bella when he told them he was tired.

He fell into his bed and closed his eyes. In the darkness of his dream-like state, he saw blue eyes staring at him. As the blue eyes got closer, he could make out antlers with twelve tine. It was the deer he had missed a few years ago, the one he saw at his mom's house the day Leonard found out he had been stealing pills. He could never forget those eyes. Maybe it was his subconscious mocking him in his weakened state.

However, the deer just stared at him with its powerful eyes, as if he was protecting Henry from something else. The shine of the antlers began to fade to black. The blue of the eyes began to go further back into the empty space. Henry felt himself drifting into a much-needed deep sleep.

- - - - -

"Henry," a voice called out, startling Henry from his sleep. The voice sounded eerily familiar. The voice spoke in a flat, medium tone with a cracky overhang and was clearly a man's voice.

"Who's there?" Henry questioned. He couldn't hear where it was coming from and he wondered if it was simply a figment of his imagination.

"Glad we finally get to talk Henry."

"Who are you?"

"We have met before, Henry. We have just never had the opportunity to talk my friend," the voice spoke very properly, but his voice still cracked in and out.

"I must be losing my mind. Am I talking to a deer? Am I dreaming?" Henry wondered, thinking back to the last thing he saw before drifting to sleep.

"No Henry, the deer has actually prevented me from speaking with you in the past. I finally 'convinced' it to let us talk." The voice answered Henry's thought, snarkily.

"How did you know what I was thinking? How does a deer prevent people from talking? What do you want? Who are you?" He asked again, not expecting the voice to reveal itself.

"Henry, Henry, Henry. I am trying to help you, my friend. Abby, Bella, Joseph, Leonard, Michelle, Thomas, they are all tired of dealing with you. They want to get rid of you. Send you away. Far away. I, however, do not want you to go. I care about you."

"If you care so much about me, why won't you tell me who you are? Why should I trust someone I don't know? Why should I trust you over my family?"

"Henry, you do know me. Unfortunately, if I told you who I was I would not be able to watch over you as well. You must trust me friend, I am here to keep you safe."

"I don't know, something doesn't feel right," Henry said, worried that he was hallucinating because of his recent anxiety. However, he also wanted to hear it out, because the thought of having someone who cared about him was refreshing.

"Something may not feel right, but does something not also feel *very* right Henry? Think about it. Your brother was so upset you were stealing his medicine that he told your mother. She and Joseph just want to live a normal life. Thomas and Bella did not think twice about leaving you here alone. And Abby.

Abby always leaves you alone, never tries to help you when you feel so alone. She does not understand what you deal with. She does not care. Me? I am always here for you. Protecting you."

Henry contemplated everything the voice had just said. It was starting to make sense. *"Leo did tell Mom about my pill problem and it makes me feel ashamed every time I'm around her. Joe doesn't believe in taking medicine and I bet he thinks this is all in my head because I'm crazy or something. Bella and Thomas did just leave me here alone, and I could see in their faces- the way their eyes seemed to glance up and down my body and the inner corner of their eyebrows raised- they both could tell something was wrong. But Abby? How could she not love me?"*

"But. How do I protect myself? I don't want to go away," Henry started, becoming more convinced of the voice's sincerity. However, he was still conflicted over the notion that Abby didn't love him.

"I am here to do that for you, Henry. I can handle them. Just do not let them get close to you. They are planning on getting rid of you tonight. Hide, do not let them near you, fight them off. I will handle the rest."

The ominous tone from the voice sent chills throughout his body. "I don't' care what they're doing! They're still family and friends. And I love Abby, I don't want them hurt," Henry said.

"Oh Henry, I would never hurt anybody. But Abby does not love you like you love her. You get too attached to people Henry. You must rebuild the wall she tore down. It was all a front put together by the others to get you to trust her so they could take you away," the voice responded. It seemed to be mocking the chills through Henry's body.

"I don't know... this just doesn't feel like it could be true," he said. He knew he was trying to convince himself more than anything. He couldn't help but to believe the voice, it seemed to really want to protect him and that's what he needed most.

"There are things we do not expect in life, Henry. People we once trusted will turn on us in a heartbeat. You have experienced this all your life. Your dad abandoned you as a child. Jessica ruined you with her desire for sex. Lisa left without a second thought to chase money. Remember all that have abandoned you. How can you expect things to change now? Let me help you Henry."

"What do I need to do," Henry meekly said, finally convinced that the voice was right.

"Just trust me Henry. Like I said, do not let them close to you. Do not trust anything they say. Let me into your heart Henry."

"Into my heart?" Henry questioned. "What does that even mean?"

"The chills you have been feeling Henry, it is me. Filling your body with my spirit. Trust me. Let me help you."

"Okay," Henry said, resigned to his fate, as he shut his eyes again and let himself feel the cold. He could finally embrace the chills.

- - - - -

The sound of voices coming from outside the apartment woke Henry again. This time Henry recognized the voices. Abby and Bella were talking. Henry reached over to grab his phone and check the time. Abby was right on schedule returning home from work.

He could barely make out what they were saying, but he could occasionally hear them mention his name. The sound of his name coming from them sent chills down his spine as he thought about what the voice told him. *"Are they going to try and kill me?"* Henry thought to himself, as his heart began to beat faster in his chest as the realization that voice may have been right become more of a reality.

"He was right. They're plotting now to take me away from here. They're tired of me," Henry thought to himself as he leaped out of bed. He ran to the front door to make sure it was locked.

"Shit, that does no good. Abby has a key," he thought to himself as he rushed frantically around the apartment trying to figure out where to hide.

"What if I lock the door to my room, turn the lights out, and get under the covers? She won't be able to get into the bedroom door if it's locked and I can play it off like I'm asleep," Henry thought to himself in a panic as he could hear Abby and Bella's conversation coming to an end.

"Great idea Henry. That will give me enough time to take care of them," the voice chimed into Henry's train of thought.

Without hesitation, Henry quietly made his way into his room, walking on his tiptoes and slowly closing the door behind him. He flicked the light off, hoping Abby wouldn't notice the light was even on to begin with. Sliding into his bed, he pulled the covers over his head and curled into a ball like a baby in the womb.

"Do not be tempted by her pleas, Henry. She will do anything to try and get you out so they can take you away."

At that moment, Henry's phone vibrated in his pocket. Looking down, he saw his mom's name appear on the screen with a text message, followed by an incoming phone call from his brother.

Henry felt his fists clenching together as he prepared for the worst. His body was becoming warm as his adrenaline kicked in and made his body go into full panic mode. *"This is it. They're trying to get me,"* Henry thought as his chest began to fill with chaos. He tossed his phone underneath his bed, however the muffled vibrations of the phone seemed louder in the silent darkness of his cover.

Henry heard the lock on the front door slowly crack as Abby inserted her key into the front door. The scream of the handle turning and the brushing of the bottom of the door swiping the floor sent chills down Henry's spine.

"This is it," Henry thought to himself as Abby closed the door silently behind her and turned the lock, cracking it back into place.

"Do not let her fool you Henry."

Henry's bedroom doorknob jiggled. The noise rang throughout the room, piercing his ears. Henry reached his hands up and slammed them against his ears, trying to prevent the rattling from entering his mind. *"Stay strong Henry,"* he told himself.

"I am here to protect you Henry. Put your trust in me."

"I am. I trust you. Please protect me," Henry thought to himself, still not sure who he was trusting to protect him but knowing that he needed protection.

"Henry?" Abby called out in her angelic voice as she knocked on the door. "Are you in there? The door is locked babe." It was hard not to answer his fiancé, her voice ringing softly and calmly into Henry's distressed mind.

"Say nothing Henry. Stay strong my friend."

Another, louder, knock came at the door. The sound of the knock hammered around in Henry's brain. He felt a migraine creeping into his head as he burrowed his brow and began to close his left eye. *"I thought you were going to protect me!"* Henry thought, trying to reach out to the voice to take his pain away.

"Dear Henry, do not be surprised at the fiery ordeal that had come onto your mind to test you, as though something damning were happening to you. Put your faith in me."

Three more rapid knocks came at the door. "Henry, wake up and let me in. Please!" Abby's once angelic voice called out to him in a distressed and tired tone.

"Remain strong, Henry."

The sound of the knocking, the despair in Abby's voice, and the ominous tone in the stranger's voice racked around in Henry's brain like the breaking of balls in billiards. *"Please stop,"* Henry cried to himself.

Then all was silent. *"What is she doing. Did she leave?"* Henry wondered to himself as the silence drug on and became more eerie as time seemed to stop in place. Henry remained still as the beating of his heart slowed down.

Ba-dump. Ba-dump. Ba-dump.

Ba-dump. Ba-dump.

Ba-dump.

The Little Drummer Boy played his tune deep within Henry's chest. He put his hands over his face to try and quiet the sound of the air flowing in and out of his nose. He did all he could to avoid making any sound in the piercing silence that had surrounded him.

The sound of metal scraping metal pierced through the cloud of silence in Henry's room. Abby had grabbed a butter knife and was trying to wiggle the door latch open.

- - - - -

"Henry, what are you doing?" Abby thought to herself. As she struggled to slide the butter knife between the doorframe and the lock, she slowly put her weight against the door in hopes of breaking the tension of the doorframe and lock free. Wiggling the butter knife up and down, Abby struggled to push the metal tip against the lock, trying to push it into the door and release its grip on the doorframe.

Abby began to bang on the door again and pleaded "Henry, please let me in!" There was only silence in response. Chills shot through her body as panic overcame her calm demeanor. She began to wiggle the butter knife between the door and lock again, more rapidly and more fiercely.

"GO AWAY ABBY!" Henry yelled from behind the door. Abby noticed something strange in Henry's voice, cracking in and out more than normal. She worked the butter knife even more hurriedly and with more force, trying harder and harder to get into the room.

217

Finally, Abby felt the lock give and heard the soft click of the lock returning to its home within the door and away from the doorframe. She pushed her weight against the door as it flung open. She immediately flipped the light switch on to see Henry bundled underneath his covers on the bed, balled up like he was hiding from something. "Henry, what is going on?" She cried.

"Henry! I told you not to let her in you fool!"

"I'm sorry! I didn't mean to!" Henry cried out, his voice trembling.

"Henry, what are you talking about? You didn't mean to what?" Abby said, quivering with tears sliding down her cheeks and the saltiness seeping in between the crease of her lips.

"Abby, I know what you're trying to do. I won't let you take me!" Henry said, pulling the covers more tightly around his body. It was becoming more difficult for him to breathe in the confined space and the covers, but he wouldn't let her take him.

"Henry," Abby started as she took a step towards Henry.

"Henry, she is getting closer. STOP HER!"

"ABBY, STOP. DON'T COME CLOSER!" Henry shouted from beneath his blankets.

Abby was trembling now. She was scared, she didn't know what to do. She had never seen Henry like this. "Henry, please…"

"GO AWAY!" Henry shouted once more.

Abby heard a knock at their front door and heard Bella calling from outside their apartment. She must have heard Henry's screams. The entire apartment complex had probably heard his screams by now. Bella was Henry's safe person, maybe she would know what to do. Abby slowly turned around to make her way to the front door.

"Henry, she is going to let Bella in."

"STOP ABBY! Don't let her in here!" Henry called out, this time in more of a fearful tone. Henry, with his eyes closed, only saw darkness. But every time the voice spoke to him, he would see flashes of light, seemingly implying that it was on his side.

Abby froze at the sound of Henry's cry. She didn't know what to do. She was scared. She put her back against the wall and slid down, her tears falling to the floor in a flood. What should she do? What *COULD* she do? This wasn't Henry. This wasn't the man she loved.

"Abby, what is going on!" Bella yelled from outside. "Let me in, please!"

"NO, YOU CAN'T COME IN!" Henry shouted out to Bella, poking his head from underneath the covers, eyes still closed to shield it from the light and Abby's gaze. "I know what you're doing Abby. I know you're trying to take me away. I won't let you."

"Henry!" Bella called through the door, banging her fist over and over again against the cool door.

"Henry," Abby said, wiping the tears from underneath her smeared eyes. "I'm not trying to take you away."

She realized now, Henry was having a bipolar episode. His paranoia was taking over. She had never seen him like this, but she had read about it. She didn't understand the things Henry went through like Bella did, but she was trying to learn.

"She is lying to you, Henry."

"Oh no, you can't fool me Abby," Henry said in a hysterical tone, half laughing half fearing. He opened his eyes to see Abby sitting on the floor with her back against the wall. The sound of Bella knocking on the door faded away. Henry, wide-eyed, stared coldly at Abby.

"Look Henry," Abby started as she slowly moved her back up the wall. "I have nothing in my hands, see?" Abby reached out her open hands and turned them in circles to show Henry she had nothing in her hands. "Look, let me take a few steps closer and talk to you. If you want me to stop, just tell me. Is that okay?" Abby hoped her calming voice would open Henry up.

"Do not let her near you, Henry."

"Okay Abby, Slowly. Keep your hands out," Henry hesitantly said, now ignoring the voice.

"Henry, what are you doing? You are not listening to me."

Abby slowly began to move towards Henry. Left foot first, the right foot stepping heel to toe of her left. Slowly, she made those tiny steps towards Henry, trying not to startle him in his fragile state. "Babe talk to me. What's going on? What has you scared?"

"Do not answer Henry."

"I know you're tired of dealing with me Abby," Henry trembled, afraid of the tone the voice now had taken on. "You, Bell, Thom, Mom, Leo, Joe, I know you are all tired of dealing with my issues. You want to send me away, but I don't want to go. I'll get out of your lives, just don't send me away."

Abby, fighting back tears, continued slowly forward. "Henry, none of us are tired of you. We all--"

"Do not listen to--"

"STOP!" Henry interrupted the conflicting voices, sliding the covers back over his head. He started breathing heavily, not sure if he feared Abby or the voice more. He wanted to hide from both, get rid of them. His mind couldn't handle the two of them at the same time, interrupting each other. Their voices were beginning to fade into one another.

"Henry, come out. I stopped, like you asked. My hands are still out. Come out and look at me," Abby pleaded.

"Do not do it, Henry."

Henry's mind seemed to fight itself, going back and forth on how to handle the situation at hand.

Finally, Henry decided that he had to make his own decisions, and not let some imaginary voice control him. He had been controlled by other people for too long and wanted to take a stand. It was time for Henry to control the thoughts his mind constantly soiled his life with, he no longer wanted to be a prisoner to his own mind.

He slowly poked his head out of the covers, revealing only his eyes and the bridge of his nose- a happy medium for both sides of his battling mind.

Abby, seeing Henry come out slightly from beneath the covers, asked "Do you want to come out any more than that?"

Henry slowly shook his head from side-to-side, not wanting to break the compromise he had made with himself.

"That's okay," Abby began. "Can I come closer?"

Henry gazed into his fiancé's eyes, trying to gauge her intent. He saw no anger, no ill-will, only worry and love beaming from her beautiful, earthy brown eyes. Henry slowly nodded his head but said, "Slow."

Abby, making the same small steps she had made before, proceeded towards Henry and began talking again. "Why do you think we are tired of you babe? We all love you."

"Do not tell her about me, Henry. They will only think you are crazier than they already do."

Henry silently contemplated the question Abby had just asked and considered what the voice had told him before he responded. "I just know," he softly said, muffled beneath the covers. His eyes gazed at Abby, still in her work uniform, makeup smeared from her eyes to the dimples on either side of her round face scattered around her freckles, worry and love radiating from her eyes, slowly making her way towards Henry's shivering body.

"We don't want to take you anywhere Henry," Abby said as she approached the bed.

A loud knock came from the door as Bella began to bang on the door again. "ABBY! HENRY! SOMEONE!" She called out.

Henry, jarred and shocked by the banging and yelling, slid his head back underneath the covers and yelled "STOP!" as Abby stopped in her tracks.

"Bella," Abby called out, hoping she could hear her from here, not wanting to lose the progress she had made. "Please, just wait."

The knocking at the door stopped, and Abby breathed a sigh of relief that Bella had apparently heard her. "Henry, babe, come back out. I got her to stop."

"Henry, stay where you are."

"Leave. Me. ALONE!" Henry cried out.

"Henry, I'm sorry. I'll back away," Abby stammered, scared that all the progress she had made was now ruined.

"No," Henry softly said as he pulled the covers from around his face fully. "Not you."

Abby stopped in her tracks, unsure of who Henry had yelled at if not her. She slowly made her way to the bed and sat down on the edge. "Is this okay Henry?" she asked.

Henry nodded and closed his eyes slowly. Abby reached her hand out and wrapped her fingers around Henry's cold hands. As her fingers wrapped around his, the heat from her hands seemed to slowly transfer to Henry. Abby looked down at Henry, with his eyes still closed, mouth slightly opened as he breathed in and out, slowly but peacefully. Henry had fallen asleep.

She leaned over and planted a light kiss on Henry's cheek, as she slowly got up and crept to the front door. As she opened the door, she saw Bella leaning against the railing in front of their door, facing the parking lot, with a line of smoke coming from her cigarette. "Bell," Abby quietly called out.

"What's going on?" Bella said, hearing Abby's quiet voice, as she turned around to see Abby's tear stained face.

"I've never seen this happen before. Henry was so convinced that we wanted to take him away, that we were tired of him. He hid under his covers and only barely came out."

"Who wanted to take him away? Why?" Bella asked, her eyes now also filled with worry and concern.

"Me, you, Thom, Wanda, Joe, Leonard. He said he 'just knew' we wanted to get rid of him," Abby said, as her eyes made their way to the ground, recounting what had happened mere minutes ago. "I really think he was having some kind of bipolar episode. He was just so paranoid. It scared me, Bell."

Bella tried to do what Thomas always did to her and looked deep into Abby's eyes. She could see the fear, the worry, but most of all she could see the love in Abby's eyes for Bella's best friend.

Abby and Bella had gotten close over the last few years as they had gotten to know each other. She had grown to love and appreciate Abby for the way she treated Henry.

"How is he now?" Bella asked.

"Sleeping. As soon as I was able to get close enough to sit down on the edge of the bed and hold his hand, he drifted off to sleep."

"Let him sleep tonight," Bella said. "You get some sleep too sweetie."

- - - - -

Henry opened his eyes and rolled over, seeing the covers where Abby normally slept ruffled and the pillow indented with where her head had been rested through the night. Henry sat up and looked around his room. He took a big whiff and smelled the scent of bacon that was wafting around the apartment.

Henry stood up, stretched his sore body, and made his way to the kitchen. He looked at Abby, wearing one of his t-shirts and a pair of his boxer shorts, a plate full of bacon next to her, and a pancake cooking in front of her. She turned around as she heard him enter and smiled, "How are you this morning, handsome?"

"I'm good," Henry replied, sitting down at the table. "I'm sorry I was asleep when you got home last night babe. I just didn't feel good last night."

Abby, spatula pressed against the hot pan as she went to flip a pancake, froze in her spot. "Henry," she began. "You were awake."

"I was?" He said back, inquisitively. "I don't remember being awake when you came in babe."

Abby stood there in shock. How could Henry not remember what happened? "Henry, are you joking?"

"No Abby," Henry said, raising one eyebrow above the other. "Why are you acting so surprised? You know I don't remember waking up half the time when you come in."

"Henry..." Abby began.

"Shit Abby," Henry said as he pushed his way out of his seat, sending it backwards towards the ground. "The spatula is on fire!" he said as he grabbed the plastic spatula melting in his fiancé's hand and threw it into the sink, running cold water over it.

"Henry," Abby said, unfazed by the smell of burning plastic entering her nose and reaching for another spatula to finish cooking their breakfast. "Sit down. We need to talk."

- - - - -

Henry sat silently, staring down at the last piece of bacon and puddles of maple syrup on his plate. He struggled to try and remember even a glimpse of what she was recounting, but nothing rose to the surface.

It scared him that this had happened, but it scared him even more that he couldn't remember it. What if it was worse next time? What if he hurt someone next time?

He looked up at Abby, with tears beginning to form in his eyes, and said "I'm so sorry."

"Henry, don't apologize," Abby said, reaching past her plate and grabbing Henry's hands. "I love you, no matter what may happen. I will always love you."

Henry looked down at Abby's soft and perfect hands, holding his rough and damaged hands. He looked back up and into Abby's eyes. Looking back at him, he saw love. He felt love. Regardless of what issues he had faced, regardless of the battles he fought, Abby really did love him through it all. "I love you, Abby."

"Always," she smiled at him.

"Forever," he smiled back, lifting her hands to his lips and softly kissing the spaces in between her knuckles.

"I love you too, Henry."

PART 6:
DUTCH
PRESENT DAY

- - - - -

Henry looked down at his glass, now full of nothing but air and ice. His broken reflection staring back at him across the surface of the ice cubes, Henry smiled at how far he had come over the last five years and the battles he had fought and won. He knew the war would never be over, but he had an army behind him that would support him in every battle he faced. He reached down and rubbed the soft fur on the top of Dutch's head, as Dutch looked up at Henry with his sky-blue eyes and a slight smile on his face.

Henry and Abby got Dutch earlier this year, and he had quickly become a companion for Henry. Henry was immediately drawn to Dutch because of his eyes. The sky-blue radiated a calming glow from within. They held a protective gaze over Henry and Abby.

His eyes reminded Henry of the deer that he had seen over the last few years, the one he saw the night he had a major bipolar episode and thought everyone was trying to get rid of him. Henry remembered one thing from that night: the deer's eyes protecting Henry before he fell asleep. Perhaps the deer was just a figment of his subconscious that tried to protect him from his own mind, but it was real to Henry.

Dutch sat up and turned towards Henry. He lifted his paw up and rested it on Henry's knee. He always seemed to know when Henry was having a bad day or was on the verge of a panic attack and would be right there to comfort him.

Dutch reached his head towards Henry and began to lick the taste of cranberry off his hand.

Henry smiled as he put the cold glass to his lips and let a piece of ice slide against his tongue. As crazy as it sounded, Dutch was a perpetual reminder to Henry that he was not alone in his battles.

A Henry bent down to put out his dwindling cigarette, he stopped and stared at the end of it burning off its last ash. Cigarettes were a reminder of death for Henry, when he smoked he would often think about how he was slowly killing himself. The way the cigarette would burn until it could burn no more reminded him of his soul, how bright it would burn within his chest until its final light went out. As Henry smashed the cigarette into the bucket seated next to him, he took in a deep breath and looked down at Dutch.

"I'm done smoking for good buddy. I have a life to live, and I don't want to take any time from it," he said.

Dutch wagged his tail and nuzzled his head against Henry's leg, as if to say that he was proud. Henry knew Dutch didn't know exactly what he was talking about, but they both sensed that the other was happy.

As Henry once more lifted the glass to his lips, he heard a low growl from Dutch, immediately followed by the creaking of a gate opening in Henry's backyard. Henry looked down at Dutch -who was now standing tall - turned towards the darkness, one of his front legs tucked under his stomach, hair standing straight up across his spine, and his blue eyes locked on something in front of him.

As Henry sat in his seat, he could her the crunch of grass as someone approached his porch. Dutch, still in his alert position, was now growling louder and more fiercely as the sound of footsteps made their way up the wooden steps of the porch. Henry looked up to see the dark outline of a man approaching.

As the man got closer, his face became clearer as it was illuminated more by the moonlight. Henry smiled as the man, nearly identical in stature to Henry and dressed in a black suit, opened his mouth and spoke **"Henry."**

"Old friend," Henry said looking into the eyes of the man standing in front of him engulfed in black.

Henry reached down to rub Dutch's head and let him know he was okay. Dutch, putting his raised leg down, and lowering the hair on his back, moved his body in front of Henry. Dutch's bright sky-blue eyes remained fixated on the where the man stood in front of him, ensuring he could not get any closer to Henry than Dutch allowed.

"Henry," the cracky voice said again. **"It has been too long, friend."**

"Actually," Henry said, "It's not been long enough." Henry laughed as the man snarled his nose up at Henry and cut his eyes towards him. Henry lifted his glass to his lips again, allowing another piece of ice to slide against his tongue. The chill of the ice felt good in Henry's mouth.

Henry held the glass up and closed one eye, as he looked through the glass to see his reflection on the other side. "I see you every morning when I look in the mirror. I see you every day when I sit alone at lunch. I see you every night when I close my eyes."

"Then why do you ignore me? We used to be such good friends," he said, taking a step towards Henry. Dutch, his growl now louder as the man approached his owner, let out a snap in the direction of the man. The man stopped in his tracks and took a step backwards, respecting Dutch's authority.

Henry gazed into the man's eyes, seeing the reflection of himself again, smirking. "I ignore you, because I am happier without you."

"Oh Henry, don't be rude. I have always been kind to you. I have always looked out for you," the man said, mockingly.

Dutch, sensing the arrogance in the man's voice, let out another deep growl to remind him he was still there to protect Henry. "It's okay buddy," Henry said, reaching over to stroke Dutch's head. Turning his attention back to the man, Henry said "This war will wage well into both of our lives, you know?"

"A war I will win Henry."

"You haven't even won a battle yet. How do you expect to win the war?" Henry laughed in the face of the man standing in front of him. "You've seen the army I have with me. The people who stand by me and fight with me. Those who fight for me. You, though. You fight alone."

The man, once again, took a step towards Henry, clearly angry with Henry's taunting. This time, Dutch took a step towards the man to back him away. **"Henry, you will not have them with you forever. Eventually it will be just me and you."**

"Maybe," Henry said, resting his now empty glass on the ground beside him and slowly standing up to be face-to-face with the man in front of him. Henry reached down to rest his hand on the velvety softness of Dutch's head. He looked down at Dutch, and back up at the man in front of him. "But for now, I am not alone."

Henry heard the screen door open and he turned to see Abby peeking her head around the door. With her bedridden hair in knots and curls, one cheek redder than the other, and sleepiness in her eyes, she said "Henry, who are you talking to?"

Dutch, hearing his mom's voice, turned and ran to her with his tail wagging as she reached down to rub his head. "Myself," Henry smiled as he turned to look at where the man had stood mere seconds ago. "Just myself Abby."

"Come to bed babe," Abby yawned. "We have a busy day tomorrow. Brunch with Bell and Thom, lunch with

Leonard, and dinner at your grandparents with your mom and Joe."

Henry turned around and looked at Abby's sleepy face. He smiled as he thought about his friends and family, all those who fought with him and for him. He knelt down and clicked his tongue against the roof of his mouth, calling for Dutch to come to him.

Dutch, turning from Abby's hand, ran to Henry and began licking his face. Dutch could tell he had been a good boy, Henry grabbed the sides of Dutch's head and ruffled his ears. "You ready for bed buddy?" Henry asked Dutch, staring into the sky-blue eyes and seeing himself smiling within them.

Made in the USA
Columbia, SC
03 May 2019